TOUCH OF CHAOS

USA TODAY BESTSELLING AUTHOR
C. HALLMAN

Copyright © 2021 Bleeding Heart Press

www.bleedingheartpress.com

Editing by Kelly Allenby

Cover Design by Opulent Cover and Design

All rights reserved.

No part of this book may be reproduced in any form or by any electronic or mechanical means, including information storage and retrieval systems, without written permission from the author, except for the use of brief quotations in a book review.

1
SCARLET

*H*uddled behind a large tree, I stay hiding from everyone passing by. Not that there are a lot of people driving out here, but I can't be sure Ren… no, River, isn't looking for me yet. Even with everything he's done, I still feel bad about leaving the way I did. I'm worried he is hurt, angry, and alone. But I know I can't help him, at least not on my own. I don't know much about split personality disorder. Really only from movies and TV shows and those never showed me how to treat it. All I know is that Ren turns into a different person, literally. A person who dislikes me very much.

Now that I think about it, I feel stupid for not seeing it before. The sudden mood changes, the seemingly forgotten conversations, the way I never got to meet River or even hear his voice. It all seems so obvious now. I guess I was blinded by love. I didn't want to believe that there was something wrong with our relationship. I waited so long to be with Ren. I didn't want to see the red flags until it was too late.

The wind blows harshly around me as the sun sets on the horizon. With my back against the rough bark of the tree, I cross my arms in front of my chest to keep warm, just as I hear the sound of car engines approaching. Carefully, I peek around the tree to the parking lot of the gas station I told my dad I would be. Only when I see the family black SVU pull up into an empty spot, do I perk up. I wait another beat before the back door opens and a large man dressed in a dark gray suit steps out. *Dad.*

Without another thought, I duck around the tree and run toward my father. He has his back turned to me, but as soon as he hears me approach, he spins around. His dark, wary eyes light up when he sees me. He opens his arms just as I slam into his chest, harshly. Burying my nose into his suit jacket, I let the familiar scent of his cologne calm me down. He wraps his strong arms around me, pulling me closer until I can barely breathe.

"Jesus, Scarlet, do you not have any idea how worried we were?" he murmurs into my hair before kissing the crown of my head, still not willing to let me go.

Usually, there is no show of affection in public. My dad has to uphold a certain image in front of his people and even the civilians. An image that doesn't allow to show any kind of emotions. My father is one of the most feared men in the state, and he prides himself on keeping it that way. But today is not a normal day, and the situation is anything but usual.

"I'm so sorry I worried you, but I promise I'm fine. I've been fine this whole time."

He gives me one last squeeze before releasing me reluctantly. I straighten up just to see my brother standing a few feet away from us.

"Hey, sis," he greets me, his eyes soft, brimming with happiness.

"Quinton." I sigh, stepping into my brother's bear hug next. "If he hurt you, I'll kill him," he whispers into my ear during our embrace.

"I know, but he didn't," I swear, barely able to get the word out while I'm getting squeezed tightly.

My brother releases me and only now do I realize how I'm shaking.

"Let's get you into the car." My father ushers me to the backseat of the SUV while Quinton takes the passenger seat.

Tony, one of my father's drivers, gives me a courtesy nod in the back mirror as I settle into the leather seat. My father slides in beside me.

"You need to tell me where he is, Scarlet. Where is Ren?" My dad questions. "I already have back up on the way to search the area."

My heart slams against my chest, thinking about what will happen if my father's men find him right now. I told Ren I don't believe my dad would kill him, but the truth is, I can't be sure what would happen, especially now. What if they find him and he is still River?

"Ren is gone," I finally say.

"Don't lie to me, Scarlet. You need to tell me the truth."

"I am, Ren is gone…" A wave of emotion overcomes me, pressure building behind my eyes as the tears start to fall down my face. My Ren is gone, and I don't know how to get him back. "We were staying together in a cabin not far from here. But when I left, he was not Ren anymore."

"What do you mean by that?" Quinton asks from the front seat.

"I mean Ren is sick. He is not himself right now. He needs help. More help than I can give him. We need to find him and help him together."

"Sick how?" My father looks at me in confusion. "What direction is the cabin?"

Before I can answer either of his questions, his phone rings in his pocket. He takes it out and looks at the screen. "It's your mother. She has been beside herself, inconsolable since you've been gone."

Guilt slithers up my spine like a poisonous snake. Even though I didn't leave by my choice, I also didn't try to get away until now.

My father hands me his phone, and I press the green button before holding the small device to my ear. "Mom?"

"Oh my god, Scarlet." My name comes out as a sigh, and I can feel my mom's relief through the phone as she quietly sobs into the receiver. "I was so worried about you. You have no idea how much I love you. If something would've happened to you…"

"Mom, it's okay. I'm here. Nothing bad happened to me. I promise. I swear I'm on my way home, and I'll explain everything to you when I get there." My words only calm her down a little, but enough to tell me again how much she loves me and that she can't wait for me to get home.

I hang up the phone as the driver starts the car and pulls out of the small and shabby parking lot. Handing his cell back to my dad, he shoves it into his pocket before bombarding me with questions once more. "What do you mean by Ren is sick? What king of sickness? Are you sure you are okay?"

"Positive. It's not the kind of thing that is contagious." I take a deep breath, not sure where to start. "I think Ren is mentally ill, like a split personality or something like that."

"No shit," Quinton grumbles from the front of the car.

"I'm serious. Ren kept talking about having a brother named River. He talked about him like he is a real person, so real that I believed him. He talked to him on the phone and on the computer, but I never saw him or heard his voice. He kept saying it wasn't the right time to meet." Though I met him today all right.

I continue to share about things that have happened, how Ren becomes a different person sometimes and how he is influenced by River, which I refer to as his bad side. I also tell them about Rebecca and her son, about New Haven, and how they are still taking children off the street. I skim over the part where Ren took me to kill someone and the trip to New Haven to kill Rebecca. Those fun facts I keep for another time. Right now, I need to get them on my side so I can help Ren.

"I don't know, Scar," my father says when I catch my breath. "I don't know a lot about this illness, and I've definitely never heard about River before. Don't you think this would have come up sooner? I can't believe someone just gets this without any prior signs."

"I'm not sure either, but we need to figure it out. We need to ask a psychologist and help him—"

"We don't have to do anything right now besides get you home to your mother," Dad insists. "Everything else can wait until tomorrow."

No, I can't wait until tomorrow. "What about you, Q? Have you ever heard Ren talk about River or seen anything that was off?"

My brother stays quiet. Instead of answering my question, he silently looks out of the window. When he finally speaks, his voice is void of all emotion. "All I know is that he was my best friend my whole life before he betrayed me in the worst way possible. I've been trying to find an explanation, any kind of hint why he would suddenly change so much. This would explain it, but just like you two, I don't really know much about this disorder. I don't think we should jump to conclusions. Either way, he tried to hurt Aspen, and I don't know if I can ever forgive him for that."

"I really do think he's sick," I say. "He's not doing this on purpose."

"I just don't want you to look for excuses. And even if you're right, and he has a split personality, it would still be him, or at least part of him, doing all these things."

My shoulders sag. Clearly, there is no reasoning with

Quinton right now. I glance at my father sitting next to me. The expression on his weathered face lets me know he is deep in thought. At least he's not dismissing me completely. All I have to do now is convince him that Ren is worth saving. I have to do it, not only to save him, but to save myself as well.

2
RIVER

That fucking bitch.
Those three words keep going through my skull on repeat as soon as I wake up on the cold, hard floor. How long have I been here? I don't have a clue. My vision's a little blurry when I first open my eyes. It's still light out, so it can't have been all that long. Long enough for her to get away, though. That stupid fucking bitch.

Because she's gone. It's like I can feel her absence, so I know I'm alone here. My head is pounding where that little slut hit me. My vision's still blurred, but getting better as I make my way to my feet. The room spins, and I have to lean against the wall to hold myself up while my stomach feels like it's flipping inside me. It takes a few slow, deep breaths to get control of the nausea, but soon I'm able to move without it feeling like I'm about to hurl my guts up.

All because of her. And because Ren lost sight of the goal. I told him we couldn't trust her, but the useless prick didn't listen to me, of course. He fucked up everything. Fucked up my plan, my revenge, my fucking life. After everything we've been through, after all of our work and the hours spent talking over every last piece of what we would both have to do, he decides to let a little cunt change his mind. Like she's his family now or some shit. Like she matters more than me. More than blood.

I always knew I was better off alone. Without a woman to fuck with my head and get my priorities screwed up. How many times did I tell him we needed to stay focused? How many times did I remind him why we started this in the first place?

Somehow, I manage to stagger to the kitchen and turn on the cold tap. Splashing my face with the icy water is like sticking tiny needles in my skin, but it's enough to wake me up a little more. I'm still fighting a brutal headache and sometimes my vision doubles, but I'm alive. It'll get better.

And once it does, I'll make sure the little bitch who did this to me regrets it until her last breath… which won't come too long after I get my hands on her. It'll only feel like an agonized eternity to her thanks to the damage I plan to do. Slowly. One cut at a time.

Cupping my hand under the tap, I catch some water and slurp it up. That helps, too. Like it wakes up my insides as it spreads through my chest. It doesn't do a damn thing to cool off my boiling rage, though. It's been boiling for too long now. It'll take a lot more than a cold drink to put it out.

Years. Most of my life. There's been a burning inside me all this time. Hatred pushes me forward. It's what keeps me breathing sometimes, when the memories are too thick and too painful and want to crush me under their weight. Those are the times hatred is my best friend. Rage. The need for revenge.

    The water feels good against the back of my neck once I splash it there before I turn off the tap. It's so quiet in here now. All I hear is the thudding of my heart. Every thud makes my head hurt that much worse, but I can't calm it no matter how much I know I should. Every time I close my eyes, I see the face of another person who's betrayed me. Another person who needs to die for what they've done.

    Though now, there is a new face, Scarlet. I like to remember her the way she was just before she hit me over the head. Wide-eyed, terrified, struggling even though there was no point. At least, that was what I thought before she taught me otherwise.

    She has to go. Not only because she gave me a lump on the back of my head, either. Not because she left me here to die. Because she turned Ren against me. Before he fucked her, it was the two of us. We had everything we needed. We had a goal, a reason to get up every day. I could forget the worst of the memories even if only for a little while, because I had something to direct my energy toward. I had my plans.

    She turned my plans into nothing. Made them useless. I put all of this together with the two of us in mind. My brother and me, the way it's always been. The two of us against everybody who ever caused us pain. And there was so much pain, wasn't there? For no fucking reason beyond the sad truth I figured out when I was way too young:

some people just like to hurt other people because they can.

Rebecca could. And she did, and so did her braindead acolytes. They only needed permission to be the worst possible versions of themselves. Cruel, cold, sadistic. They told themselves it was God's will or whatever it took to help them sleep at night. After a while, I bet, they didn't have to bother with that. They slept soundly without having to justify their cruelty.

How many nights did Christian spend sleeping well while one or more of us shivered and wept in the dark?

Here's the thing about that. Something he never figured out. I doubt Rebecca did, either, since she's got the imagination of a fucking fruit fly: you hurt somebody enough times and leave them locked in the dark to get over it, and eventually they learn to stop dwelling on the pain. A defense mechanism at first. A way to cope with the sort of shit that would break an adult's brain, much less a kid's.

Over time, they turn their thoughts away from their agony and toward the people responsible. They start to think. Plan. Hate. They imagine what it would be like if the positions were reversed. If the person who humiliated them, tortured them, broke them down was the one on their knees begging for mercy.

Give it enough time, and imagining isn't going to do the trick anymore. It's time for action. And all those vivid fantasies can come to life.

Even now, with my head threatening to split in two with every tentative step I take toward the kitchen table, I have to grin at the memory of Christian's terror. There's never been a more satisfying moment in my entire life than the moment he realized all the pain he'd ever inflicted was about to come back ten times over. I look down at my hands and can still see them coated in his warm, sticky blood. The memory makes my cock twitch and my chest swell with satisfaction. I wish I could do it all over again, I really do. A piece of shit like him deserves to die more than once, and I sure as hell deserve to be the one to make it happen.

Killing Christian was a drop in the ocean, though. One piece in a much larger puzzle. He might have taken sickening pleasure in what he did to those of us cursed by his presence in our lives, but he wasn't acting on his own. He had his orders. Somebody granted him power over us.

Rebecca's face and her snide, holier-than-thou smirk replace Scarlet's image at the forefront of my mind. This is all her fault. She started this. She is a fucking cunt who needs to die slowly and painfully. Her son will die even slower for what he has done. Following his mother's footsteps, taking kids off the street, abusing and grooming them before selling the poor souls to the highest bidder.

I won't stop at destroying New Haven, either. I'm going to burn down the entire world for what they did to me. I don't need Ren or anyone else. Hell, I'd rather be alone, since I'm apparently the only person I can count on. Fuck Ren and his little bitch of a girlfriend. Fuck them all.

There I was, figuring the living hell we both suffered through would be enough to bind us together forever. That at least there was one person in the world I didn't need to explain myself to. One person who understands. How naive could I be? How trusting? I should've known somebody would come along and steal his attention and his loyalty.

My teeth grind together at the thought of his betrayal. My own brother. I'm doing this for both of us—can't he see that? No, he's blinded by a tight pussy and a nice pair of tits.

He needs to know what he's done. How he's betrayed not only me but everybody like us. Everyone who knows the pain and humiliation we went through. The ones who are too weak to fight back. The ones who never got a chance to grow up and decide for themselves whether they wanted to be part of Rebecca's sickness.

I grab a hold of the pen and start scribbling down a letter to my dear brother on the back of a piece of scrap paper.

R<small>EN</small>,

Scarlet ran off. I tried to stop her, but she hit me across the head and left me for dead. The only good thing about her was her mouth when it was wrapped around my cock in the shower. She didn't like the way I fucked her throat, though. Even cried a little. She needs some better training, if you ever see her again.

Since you fucked up so royally last time, I will move forward without you. Don't contact me again.

H<small>OPE TO SEE YOU NEVER</small>,
River

. . .

Maybe I should've gone into detail about everything I did to his precious Scarlet. It would give him something to reflect on the next time he decides to betray me. Oh, who am I kidding? There won't be another betrayal because I can't afford to trust him again. I meant it when I said I'm leaving him behind. Cutting the dead weight free. Let him see how far he gets without me keeping him focused. Let him see who will take him back now that he's fucked over every other person he was ever close to. Quinton and his precious family, for instance. He has nowhere to go now. He's going to figure out in no time what a massive mistake he made, crossing me.

I throw the pen across the room, so fucking tired of this shit. Everyone is against me. It's all fucking hopeless. I have no one. I'm destined to be alone forever and always.

One thing I know for certain, I won't stop until they've all paid. Revenge will be mine, even if it's the last thing I ever do.

3
SCARLET

I'm surprised Mom doesn't break the window so she can get to me quicker once we come to a stop in front of the house. Now that I know I'm safe and there isn't that whole adrenaline rush, fight-or-flight thing going on, I'm completely wiped out. My limbs are heavy enough that I'm sure I won't be able to get out of the SUV on my own.

I guess I'm not moving fast enough for her. Once she yanks the door open, she pulls me from the vehicle with Dad helping, nudging me in her direction. "Oh, my god!" she sobs before breaking down into unintelligible babble. Now she's holding me close, shaking, rocking me back and forth like I'm a baby. "Oh, honey. Oh, I've been so worried. We've all been so scared for you."

"I'm sorry for all of that. I didn't want to scare you." It's feeling her physical reaction that makes it real. Her trembling, the way she squeezes me until I'm pretty sure she's going to crack my ribs. Her short, sharp little breaths that stir my hair and warm my skin.

I'm home. Having my mother's arms around me means I'm home. I didn't realize until now that Mom has her own particular smell—it's her Chanel No. 5, the same perfume she's worn all my life. It clings to her clothes, her hair, and her skin and smelling it takes me back to so many happy memories.

I open my eyes and notice Aspen standing a few feet away. Her eyes shine with tears as she offers me a faint, shaky little smile. "It's good to see you." She's trying to sound upbeat and positive. That's how she is. But I can see through her. And I feel terrible when I think of her waiting here for any word from me the way I know Mom must've been. It's not like I didn't think about her at all while I was gone—I knew there were people at home, probably out of their minds with worry. Funny how it was easier to gloss over that when all that mattered was being with Ren. It wasn't that I didn't care. It was just that I told myself it was for the best that we were together, the way we were supposed to be.

I shudder a little when I think back on that. I had no idea what I was dealing with. Not the slightest clue what Ren was really going through.

I can't think about that right now, since I don't want to, like, break down in front of anybody. As it is, I know damn well I'll pretty much be locked away after this. Not as punishment, but out of concern.

When Aspen hugs me, once Mom finally lets me go, the presence of a bump between us almost comes as a surprise. It wasn't so pronounced the last time I saw her. Another reminder of how much time has passed.

And another reminder of what's growing inside me.

"How are you feeling?" I ask her as we walk arm in arm up to the house. I've never been so glad to see it, and to know I'll be comfortable tonight.

But Ren won't. I can't think about that. I don't know if I'll be able to stop crying.

"Me?" She blurts out a little laugh and shakes her head. "I am not the person who matters the most right now."

"I would argue with that," Quinton pipes up behind me.

"Of course you would." She gives him a little grin over her shoulder as we step through the door. It's warm and familiar, and all of a sudden, I want nothing more than a shower. I need to wash everything away and start fresh. Maybe I'll be able to think a little clearer once I do.

"I mean it, though. How have you been? How are things with the baby?" I ask her.

"Absolutely fine." She gives me another little squeeze when we reach the foot of the stairs. "Even better now that you're back."

"Why don't you go up, get yourself some rest once you've cleaned up a bit?" My father stands surprisingly close to me, but then everybody does. They cluster around me in a tight little circle like they're afraid I'll get away if they don't cage me in. Even more of a reason to keep things to myself, especially the baby. It's bad enough I doubt I'll be allowed outside for a while—after everything I put my parents through, I'd better get used to the sight of my bedroom walls.

Instead of going straight upstairs, I look up at him. "We can't forget him," I whisper. "Please."

Something stormy passes over his face and hardens his features. I recognize this expression, and it makes my heart sink. There's not much getting through to him when he feels this way. "Scarlet, this isn't the time."

"You're not going to get much sympathy out of any of us right now," Quinton growls. From the corner of my eye, I watch Aspen put a hand on his shoulder, but I doubt she'll be able to get through to him. He's just like Dad. Once he makes up his mind, that's it.

"He's sick." I lift my chin and look around, searching for understanding. An ally. "I know how you feel about it. You already told me in the car. But he needs help. Okay, so maybe there's part of him that knows he's doing these things, although, I doubt it," I add when Q's flashing eyes meet mine. "I swear. He becomes a different person. The way he made it sound, he really thought River was... I don't know, a separate entity. I don't know how to explain it." Frustrated tears fill my eyes, but I blink them back. This isn't the time to break down. Not when Ren needs me.

"You're tired." Dad glances at Mom, who puts an arm around my waist. "Get some rest. We'll talk about this once you've pulled yourself together a little."

In other words, run off like a good little girl. There's not much I hate more than being dismissed that way, and it's something Dad is an expert in. He knows just how to make a person feel childish and patronized.

"Let's go," Mom murmurs. "You need to take care of

yourself. If Ren does need you, he'll need you to be at your best. You won't do him any good if you're sick and exhausted."

She doesn't get it. None of them do. They would rather treat me like I'm some fragile thing that's going to break. I don't have a choice but to let her lead me upstairs. Maybe I'll be able to get through to them tomorrow. Either way, I have to try.

IF IT WASN'T for Mom barging into my room, I would probably keep pacing my room while plotting how to help Ren. I feel sick to my stomach, and every move only makes the nausea worse. So this is what I have to look forward to. Worried every minute about the father of my baby while the baby makes me sick every morning. I know I'm not alone, not really, but it feels that way.

"Come on now," she urges in a bright voice. "We're going to have visitors." She moves as she speaks, fluttering around the room like a hummingbird. Opening the blinds, filling the room with blinding sunshine.

"Who?" I even sound sick and miserable. She can't know. Nobody can know. I clear my throat and try again. "Who's coming over?"

"Roman and Sophie," she tells me as she picks up the clothes I left in a pile before getting in the shower yesterday, then collapsing into bed. "And they're bringing Luna."

The mention of Luna is a candle flickering to life in my

heart. If there's anybody I can count on to understand, it's her. She'll listen. She'll want to help her brother.

"Also…" Mom perches on the side of the bed, twisting her hands in her lap before she can't help but reach out to stroke my hair. "I understand your father was busy all night getting to the root of Ren's situation. He'll want to see you when you come downstairs. You should do that soon, before the others get here. And you need to eat," she adds in a firm voice before standing.

The thought of food makes me want to cry. "I feel a little queasy," I venture. "I don't know if I want to eat."

"You have to eat a little something. Maybe some peppermint tea will help settle your stomach. I'll put on the kettle for you, but you have to come down and get it yourself."

It isn't the idea of tea that gets me going. It's wanting to know what Dad found out. It's enough to make me go through the motions of getting dressed, brushing my hair; the whole deal before I slowly make my way downstairs.

Where is Ren now? I couldn't have hit him hard enough to kill him, but who knows? No, he was breathing before I left… wasn't he? My stomach lurches, but this time it's not morning sickness that does it. I need to get a hold on myself, or I'm going to unravel. *One step at a time.*

The first step is taking the tea Mom offers, freshly brewed by the time I reach the kitchen. "Some toast, too," she insists, placing a plate on the quartz countertop. It's the last thing I feel like doing, but I pick up a slice and take one small bite, then another. I chew slowly and sip the tea, and after a few slow breaths, it seems like I'll be able to keep it down.

I have to leave the rest of the toast behind, but I take the tea with me to Dad's study. The door is open, but I knock anyway when I see him leaning in close to his MacBook screen, like he's engrossed in whatever he's reading.

His head snaps up when he hears me, and right away, he closes the machine. "Something I'm not supposed to see?" I ask, and even though I try to make it sound like I'm joking, I'm not. I sort of feel like I have to tiptoe around after scaring everybody for so long, but I'm not going to magically be okay with him treating me like a child who can't handle facts.

He scowls but nods to one of the chairs in front of him. "Take a seat. We need to talk." Once I do as he says, he sighs. "I spent hours digging into information on Safe Haven, from before we took them down. I thought I knew everything about it, really. Of course, there's never knowing everything about a place like that. So many secrets were buried." His voice cracks a little, and it's like somebody took a scalpel to my heart and sliced it open.

"Tell me," I urge, setting the mug on his desk when my hands begin to shake.

"It was your uncle Luke who gave me the answers I needed." A look of pain and disgust sweeps over his face before he pulls himself together. "As it turns out, there was a River. He did exist."

I sit up a little straighter and would swear every nerve in my body is humming. I can almost hear it in my head. River was real. Past tense. "And? Who was he? What happened to him?"

It's obvious he doesn't want to say it in the way he grinds his teeth, the way his jaw ticks. "River was Ren's biological brother."

"Was?" I whisper. "Is he… dead now?"

"I'm afraid so. Apparently, according to Luke, River died there. He couldn't remember the exact details, but it's no secret to us that children were abused, sometimes severely. Whatever was done to River was too much, and he died… while Ren was present. Luke thought Ren was too young to remember." If he knows anything else, he keeps it to himself. Maybe he wants to protect me from it.

Somehow, I knew. At least I had a good feeling it was something like this. Something that broke Ren, something so horrible his brain couldn't handle it. "That's what did it," I conclude. "That's what started it."

"We don't know that for sure," Dad tells me. "We can't pretend to be psychiatrists. But it does seem if anything could split a person's personality the way you've described Ren, that would be it. He simply couldn't handle the trauma, and his mind had to protect itself somehow."

I can't process it. My poor Ren. Imagine witnessing something like that at such a young age. "Thank you for at least humoring me enough to look into it," I tell him once my brain starts moving again, once I've shaken off the shock.

He tips his head to the side. "If anything, I wanted to know for myself why he betrayed us. Not for his sake, but for my own. Now…" He sinks back into his chair and shrugs. "I don't know what there is to be done for him, or if there's anything we can do at all. There might be no getting through to him. It could be he's completely lost touch with reality."

I can't believe that, and I won't. I am not giving up on him, though I know better than to say those words out loud. Something tells me he knows anyway when he sighs before his shoulders sag.

All of that is lost when voices echo down the hall. I'm barely out of the study before Luna throws her arms around me, followed by her parents. I can barely make out their questions since they all overlap until it's nothing but noise in my ears.

"I'm okay." That's all I can say over and over. It isn't easy to look Ren's parents in the eye after everything that happened, though when I do, there's nothing but concern reflected at me. "I'm fine. I'm not hurt or anything like that. I'm really okay." I wish I could say the same for Ren.

Dad clears his throat behind us. "Roman, Sophie. Come, have a seat. We need to talk." The two of them exchange what seems like a nervous glance before joining my father, the three of them murmuring as they enter the study.

I wait until they're inside with the door closed before pulling Luna in by her shoulders. "I need your help," I whisper, leaning in close to her ear. "We need to find Ren. He's sick, and he needs help, and right now I'm the only one who cares."

"That's not true," she whispers back, shaking her head. "I want to help him. We all do."

"What have you heard?"

She bites her lip. "Mom and Dad were talking. Something

about him having something wrong in his head. That's it. No specifics. Is it really that bad?"

All I can do is nod. "I have to get to him, and I have to tell him he needs help. Otherwise, he could get himself killed. None of this is his fault. You have to believe me."

"I do." Her eyes shine when she takes my hand and squeezes tight. "I know he wouldn't do this unless there was something really wrong."

"You'll help me?"

"I'll do everything I can."

"Girls?" Mom finds us and begins walking our way. "Are you hungry? Scarlet, you didn't finish your toast."

"We'll talk about it later," I whisper before we follow Mom toward the kitchen. I still feel like shit, which is putting it mildly, and every second that passes has me a little more worried about Ren and what he's going through.

But somebody is on my side. I have to cling to that tiny scrap of hope. Right now, it's all I have.

4
SCARLET

A few days later, and we're still not any closer to a solution. Luna and her parents are staying here, hoping to figure something out together. Ren hasn't tried to contact me and that worries me above all. What if I hit River too hard? No, I can't think about that. I won't let my mind go there. I have to believe he's still at the cabin waiting for me to come back.

A knock on my door drags me out of my thoughts. "Come in!" I Yell, loud enough for the person on the other side to hear.

The door opens, and my father appears in the doorframe. "Someone is here to talk to us."

I immediately perk up. "Who is it?"

"It's a psychologist. I'm hoping she can shine some light on our situation."

Jumping off my bed, I don't care that I'm still in my pajamas at 11 o'clock in the morning or that I've been sulking in my room for the past two days. "I'll get dressed and be right down."

My dad nods and closes the door behind him before I quickly get dressed to meet him out in the hallway. Together, we walk downstairs to his office, where a tall blonde woman is waiting for us.

She gets up from her chair as we enter.

"Hello, you must be Scarlet," she greets me, holding out her right hand for me to shake. "I'm Dr. Stone. I'm a licensed psychologist specializing in dissociative identity disorder."

"Dissociative identity disorder?" I repeat while taking her hand.

"Yes, that's the clinical term. You might know it as multiple personality or split personality disorder," she explains with a bright smile on her red painted lips.

"Please sit," my dad offers as he takes his own seat behind his large wooden desk.

Dr. Stone sits down, and I take the seat next to her.

"Dr. Stone, could you tell us a little more about this disorder?" my father asks.

"Of course. Dissociative identity disorder or DID for short is a very rare mental disorder that affects less than 2% of the entire population. It's more common in women, but men can definitely suffer from it as well. People who have DID will have at least two very distinct personalities. Some have up to one hundred personalities inside of them."

"One hundred?" I ask, astounded by the sheer number.

"It's rare, but yes, there are cases documented with these

numbers. Though it's more common to have two to ten personalities."

"Ren has two. He calls the other one River," I explain.

Dr. Stone takes a notebook and pen from her purse and lays them on her lap. She opens the book and scribbles down something on the paper.

"Would the person not know they have DID?" My dad questions.

"Not necessarily. Some patients do, some don't. The mind is a tricky thing, Mr. Rossi, and DID often comes along with a few other symptoms like memory loss, hallucinations, and delusions. It is possible that neither of the personalities knows or that only one of them does."

"Ren doesn't know; he believes River is real. He even talks to him on the phone. I don't know if River realizes it or not. I only interacted with him a few times. I think he only called himself River once in front of me."

Dr. Stone nods while she continues to write stuff down on her paper. "Usually, the separate personalities will be very distinct, with unique character traits and even mannerisms."

"Yes, I have noticed that. Ren is always kind, easygoing, and fun. River is almost the complete opposite of that. He is angry, distraught, and very hard to reason with."

Dr. Stone keeps nodding like everything I'm saying makes complete sense to her while my father seems to be unhappy about this new revelation. Or maybe he doesn't agree with my description of Ren. I'm sure we'll have a conversation about it later.

"That all sounds pretty textbook DID to me. Often a

person creates a new personality or alter ego, if you will, to personify all the feelings they don't want to feel or maybe they just can't handle them. Of course, I can't make an official diagnosis without actually talking to the patient."

My father clears his throat. "As soon as we find him, you'll be able to talk to him in person."

I suck in a deep breath, relieved that my dad seems to want to help Ren and not kill him. I let that breath out slowly, getting ready for the biggest question of all.

"Is it treatable?" I ask hopefully.

"Yes," Dr. Stone confirms, and I feel like a huge weight is lifted off my chest. My fear was that there's nothing we can do about this. That Ren will forever be trapped by the demons that haunt him.

"DID can be treated with both medication and therapy," she explains. "The most successful treatment is always to find the cause. DID is triggered by trauma and resolving that trauma is the best chance of treatment. It's usually a lifelong process, and it highly depends on how willing the patient is."

"He'll be willing to work with you," I state, not because I know it but because I have to believe it. I have to believe that Ren will try for me... for us.

"I'm glad to hear that," Dr. Stone gives me a warm smile. "Do you have any other questions for now?"

"I can't think of anything at the moment."

"Dr. Stone, thank you for coming on such short notice. I'm sure you have to get back to your other patients." My father gets up from his seat and walks around his desk. "I will be in touch."

Dr. Stone mimics my dad; quickly gathering her stuff, she gets up from her seat to shake his hand.

I, on the other hand, don't have it in me for any pleasantries at the moment. Too many thoughts running rampant in my mind. I stay seated and watch Dr. Stone exit my father's office. I'm sure my dad paid her well above her fee to be here, so I don't feel bad about being rude.

"Feeling a bit better now?" my father asked.

"Yes. My biggest fear was that there is nothing we can do to help him."

"I hope you realize that if it was anyone else—"

"He would be dead right now," I finish my father's sentence. "Trust me, I'm well aware. Why do you think he is so scared to ask you for help? I told him we should call you, but he was worried you wouldn't give him a chance to talk. He also believes you knew about New Haven."

"I didn't know."

"If you would have known, would you have done something about it?"

"Probably not," my father answers without hesitation or remorse. "I'm not a hero, Scar. You know I'm not a good guy."

I knew this, of course, but it still hurts to hear it sometimes. I know there is good inside of my father by the way he treats my mother and me, but beyond that, he is still the head of the mafia, and they're not the good guys.

"Am I interrupting?" my brother's voice startles me.

"Back so soon, Son," Dad greets Quinton.

"I figured you guys miss me so much when I'm not here."

I roll my eyes at my brother. He's always so full of himself. He's lucky that I love him. I get up from my chair, about to give him a welcoming hug, when he gives me a weird look.

"I need to talk to Dad... alone."

"About what?" I question. "Why can't I be in here? Is this about Ren?"

Quinton sighs. "Yes, it's about Ren. Which is exactly the reason you should leave."

"When are you going to stop treating me like a child?" I look between my brother and my father accusingly. "You know I'm a grown-up, right? I deserve to be part of this."

"Scar, if Q thinks it is better you don't hear this then——"

Once again, I interrupt my dad. If I were anyone else, I would be regretting my insubordination by now. "Does Quinton have a microchip implanted under his skin?"

"What does that have to do with anything?" he asks, like he doesn't already know.

"It has to do with everything. You always treat me differently than Quinton just because he is a guy."

"Everything I do is to keep you safe."

"No, everything you do is to control me," I yell. "Which is exactly the reason I didn't try to contact you sooner."

"That's not true. I don't control anything you do, but maybe I should." My father's dark eyes turn hard, and I know my outburst needs to come to an end, or I will be in real trouble.

I lower my voice. "How can you be so blind to this?" I look to my brother for any kind of reassurance that he is on my side. When Quinton averts his gaze to somewhere on the bookshelf behind me, I know I've lost him too.

"Fine, have it your way," I snap, before spinning around and storming out of my father's office.

A few treacherous tears escape the corner of my eyes as I stomp down the long hallway until I make it to Luna's room. She is the only one I can count on right now. Raising my arm, I knock on the wood softly. Loud enough for Luna to hear, but quiet enough so she will be the only one.

She opens the door a moment later, looking at me with curious eyes. "Oh, hey. Come on in." She opens the door further, and I slipped in beside her. "What's up? Any news about Ren?"

"Yes and no," I tell her. "There's no news about his whereabouts, but I talked to a psychologist, and she confirmed that he is showing signs of a split personality. She also says that it's treatable and that she can help him."

"That's amazing," Luna says, relief in her soft voice.

"So I have a confession to make," I tell her, feeling a bit guilty. "You know how I told everyone I wouldn't be able to find the cabin again?"

"Yes," she answers, drawing out the three-letter word.

"That was a lie. I know exactly where the cabin is. I was just scared of what my dad would do if he got his hands on Ren without letting me explain properly."

"Why aren't we telling him now?"

"Because I still don't trust him completely. I love my dad, but he acts before he thinks, and I'm worried he'll make Ren worse instead of helping him. If I could just talk to him, explain what is happening and that my dad isn't out to kill him, I think I could calm him down and have him come in on his own."

"I don't know, Scar. I love my brother more than anything, but he is as hardheaded as your dad."

"I can get to him. You know I can."

Luna bites her bottom lip as her light blue eyes wander all over the room like she has to really think this through. "All right, what's your plan?"

"I knew I came to the right person." I grin. "So, I'm thinking we can swipe one of the guards' cars and drive out to the cabin ourselves.

"Steal a car?"

"Not steal… borrow." I grin even wider. "You know my dad has cars ready on a whim, unlocked and key inside. This compound is so secure, no one is going to worry about their car getting stolen."

"Actually…" Luna runs her hand through her long blonde hair. "I know where my dad parked, and he leaves his keys in the glove compartment. So, we could *borrow* my parent's car. Somehow, I would feel better about that. Plus, if Ren sees my dad's car coming, he is way less likely to freak out and run."

"You are a genius, Luna! I didn't even think of that." I try to keep my voice down, but excitement has me raising my tone. I force myself to lower my volume. "So that means you are in?"

"Let's go on an adventure." Luna grins from ear to ear, but her elation doesn't reach her eyes. I find the same worry I'm feeling reflecting back at me.

"I'm a little scared too," I admit, "but it will be worth it. We'll find him and get him the help he needs."

Luna bobs her head up and down, her smile fading away. "I really hope so."

Me too.

"I'm going to go back to my room and wait. Meet me downstairs at ten tonight?"

"Sounds good," Luna answers before I slip out of her room and close the door behind me.

I make my way back to my room to take a much-needed shower before I take my time getting changed into some dark skinny jeans and a comfortable hoody. I put my unruly long hair in a bun at the top of my head and slip into my boots to complete my car-hijacking-look.

Time passes slowly for the rest of the day as I wait for ten o'clock to come around. My mom has dinner sent up to my room when I don't come downstairs to eat. I force the food down, knowing I need to feed myself and the baby. When I finally sneak down the stairs, Luna is already waiting for me at the bottom.

"Let's use the kitchen door out to the terrace and walk around to where the cars are parked," I whisper, knowing that guards are standing in front of the main door.

We tiptoe through the dark hallway and into the kitchen. My heart is racing, though I know this house like the back of my hand, I keep thinking I'm about to run into something to make a loud noise that will alert everyone under this roof.

When we get to the kitchen door, I open it slowly, expecting some kind of alarm to go off even though I know the door is not triggered. My mind is playing tricks on me, the guilt of leaving again weighing heavy on me.

Luna is right behind me as we sneak out onto the terrace and around the house onto the small gravel parking lot.

"There it is." Luna points at a dark gray SUV, and we quickly make our way over there.

Just like Luna predicted, the doors are unlocked. I slide into the driver's seat while Luna gets in on the passenger side.

"Do you even have a driver's license?" Luna asks, while digging the key from the glove compartment.

"No, but Quinton lets me drive sometimes," I admit. "It's really not that hard." I downplay the situation.

"Okay, I trust you," Luna says, as she hands me the keys.

For the first time tonight, I'm second-guessing involving Luna in my plan. She trusts me, but do I trust myself to do this? What if I mess up? What if I'm wrong, and Ren isn't there anymore… or worse, River is?

"Are you sure you want to come? I'm gonna be honest with you. I asked you to because I'm a little scared to go by myself. But I don't want to put you in any danger," I say, though I know I'm already too late.

"Stop acting like you had to drag me away. I wanna come with you. I want to find Ren just as much as you do. He is my brother, after all. My only constant. You know, I love my parents, but the bond I have with Ren is different. He is the only person who was there before I can remember, before Sophie and Roman adopted us. I couldn't bear losing him."

An image of small Ren and tiny Luna, all alone in that

cult, enters my mind. Both anger and sorrow swirl around in my gut. They had to protect themselves, just like that little boy we saw when we went to New Haven. Pressure builds behind my eyes, and I have to will the tears away before they run down my face.

Without another word, I enter the key into the ignition and turn until the engine roars to life. Putting the car into drive, I ease my foot onto the gas. *Here goes nothing.* I slowly maneuver the car out of the parking spot and onto the small road leading to the main gate of the compound.

"The guard at the gate knows my dad's car. He normally waves us through right away."

"That's what I was hoping for." It's much easier to get out of this place than in. Still, my heart beats rapidly against my chest and a sheen of sweat appears on my forehead as we approach the gate.

I slow down when the guard steps out of the guardhouse to see what car is coming. When he realizes who it is, or who he thinks it is, he waves at us before pushing the button to open the gate automatically.

Luna and I both sigh heavily in relief as we quickly make it through the gate onto the open road.

"I can't believe we did that." Luna giggles. "My parents are going to kill me, but like you said, it will be worth it."

"Yes, it will be," I agree, as I rev the engine to put more distance between us and my father's compound.

The drive takes about an hour and a half, but it feels like an eternity. Neither mine nor Luna's phone has rung, which means no one knows we're missing yet. When we finally get to the same road that the man picked me up from when I left the cabin, I park the car off to the side.

"I think you should wait here and let me go first," I blurt out. "And if you don't hear from me in thirty minutes, you'd better call our parents."

"Are you sure?" Luna asks, definitely not convinced by my new plan.

"Yes, I've been thinking about it the whole drive over here. It's the safest thing to do."

"Are you sure you're going to find your way back to the cabin in the dark?" It's a valid question, one I actually asked myself as well.

I'm pretty sure I went straight down the hill, but I have the flashlight on my phone to give me light. Plus, the sky is pretty clear today, so it's not pitch black outside, anyway.

"All right," Luna finally says. "I'll wait here, but I'll set my alarm for thirty minutes. I won't wait any longer while you are out there by yourself."

"Fair enough." I grab my phone and turn on the flashlight before getting out of the car. "Lock the door behind me," I order before slamming the car door shut.

The wind blows harshly around me, but I enjoy the fresh scent of the outdoors as I track through the forest up to the cabin. Every few minutes I check my time, making sure I'm not close to the thirty-minute mark. It only takes me twenty minutes before the familiar cabin appears between the trees. My heart sinks when I don't see a light coming from inside. It's unlikely that Ren is already asleep. But I don't want to lose hope yet.

Closing the distance between me and the cabin, at a fast pace, I reach for the door handle, hoping it will open for me. I push the handle down and sigh in relief when it gives way with ease. I push the wooden door open and take a step inside the cabin.

"Ren? It's me, I'm alone," I call out, And I'm met with silence. Still, I'm not ready to admit that he isn't here. "I'm sorry I left, but I'm back now. Please, Ren, I just want to help you."

The silence is deafening. I hang my head low in defeat. "He is gone," I whisper to myself.

"You are too late," an unfamiliar voice says behind me.

I spin around, ready to defend myself from any threat, but like the man says, I'm too late.

Something hard hits my head and the last thing I remember is my knees giving out as darkness engulfs me.

5
SCARLET

It's the violent jolt that wakes me up. Like I'm in a car or something, and we just hit a pothole nobody bothered slowing down for. My whole body bounces hard enough to bring me out of the deep darkness I was floating in a minute ago. Why did they have to wake me up? It was better to be asleep.

No. Not asleep. The throbbing in the back of my head brings everything back all at once. I wasn't asleep. I was unconscious. Because somebody hit me hard enough to make me that way.

Instinct tells me to keep my eyes closed and stay limp and still as I try to piece things together. Where am I? Who am I with? Why the hell can't I move my hands or feet?

That last question I can answer easily. I might have a bump on the back of my head—I can't reach it, but I'm guessing based on how much it hurts—but I'm not totally out of it. They tied me up. They dumped me in a van. At least that's what I'm guessing it is since I'm stretched out full length and there's still plenty of room around me when the van hits another bump, and I roll without meaning to. It's an old van, by the sound of it, creaking and groaning.

It turns out I'm surprisingly sharp when my life is in danger and my head is about to explode.

Who would have a reason to knock me unconscious, tie me up, and throw me into a van? I can only come up with one answer, and it stirs nausea in my stomach. A cold, sick sweat coats the back of my neck when I understand what this is about. Who is behind it.

I guess Ren wasn't as careful as he thought when hiding us from Rebecca once we escaped that hell on earth. I can't believe we ever went there to begin with. Another one of River's brilliant ideas that's probably going to get me killed. And there I was, having no clue what was really happening. What it was all about. Ren watched his brother die at New Haven. I don't blame him for wanting revenge. I only wish he had been in his right mind when he decided to launch an attack. Maybe he wouldn't have launched it at all. Maybe we could have worked toward helping him move past all that trauma and pain.

Instead, these monsters are still out there, doing things like this.

"Stop pretending." A sharp, nasty voice rings out, surprisingly close to where I'm lying. Male, raspy, like a smoker's voice. "There's no way you're still out cold. Not when we've been on the road all this time."

A second deep male voice adds, "Let her pretend. She won't be able to pretend for long. Not once Rebecca gets a hold of her."

Big surprise. They're taking me back. Back to New Haven, back to Rebecca, back to everything I foolishly told myself we escaped. So long as the group, the compound, and the people behind it survive, there is no escape. I don't blame the normal people who got suckered into thinking they found what they were looking for—it's not their fault, even if they have to be blind not to see what's really happening. I can't blame them for not being able to leave, even if they do understand who Rebecca really is.

For all I know, plenty of them have tried to leave and are now six feet underground. I'd bet anything on it.

I very much blame people like the ones taking me back. It will be a cold day in hell before I can muster an ounce of sympathy for them. They might be trapped just like everybody else, but they don't have to take sick joy from it.

"I wonder what Rebecca will do to her first," one of the men muses with laughter running under his words. Nasty, brutal, barely human. "A few days without food or water should break her down a little."

"I think she'll go straight for corporal punishment," the other man announces, and he's just as gleeful as his little buddy. "I wonder how many lashes she'll get with the whip. I hope it's a lot."

"She won't be so full of herself once Rebecca is finished with her." The two of them share a nice laugh while I do everything I can to pretend they're not getting to me. That's the last thing I should show them. My eyes are still closed, and my face is as blank as I can manage.

I need to get out of this, but I can't imagine how I'll do it. No way is Rebecca going to let me walk around free now that she's got her hands on me. I'll be locked away. Only Ren knows where this place is, and he's not going to come and rescue me.

How will anybody know what happened?

What a time for me to remember fighting with Dad about that tracker being in me. I guess it doesn't take a genius to know why that would come to mind right now, as I'm being driven further and further away from my home. Ren thought he was doing the right thing by taking it out, but I really wish he hadn't as the van bounces down the road, and I feel every single jolt in my joints and my throbbing head. Dad is never going to be able to find me out here.

If I ever get out of this, I'll listen to him. From now on, if he tells me to do something, I'm going to do it. Obviously, he knows better than I do, since I doubt he would ever get himself into a situation like this. Abducted, taunted, and… whatever Rebecca has in store for me.

"It always feels good when a sinner gets what's coming to them," the raspy voice announces, and the two of them laugh again. "I'm just glad I'm here for it. You don't get to bring a sinner to justice every day."

"Now, now. Remember. That's not how we're supposed to look at this." There's still a sick, twisted glee in the other man's voice. He's the driver, judging from the position of where the sound comes from. If I was talking to him, I might tell him to slow down a little. Maybe avoid a bump or two.

"We're bringing one of the sheep back to the flock."

That's too much. In the middle of all of this, it's the hypocrisy behind that sentence which breaks my silence.

"I'm not one of your sheep."

All right, maybe I shouldn't have said it, but what am I supposed to do? Lie here and let them make a joke out of me? At least I'm not whimpering and crying, which I will be damned if I ever do in front of them or anybody else. They haven't broken me, and they never will. I'm Xander Rossi's daughter, dammit. The thought stiffens my spine a little and gives me more confidence.

Confidence that dissolves when the men burst out laughing. "Like that matters," the driver tells me with another laugh that makes me grit my teeth and wish I could snap his neck. "You strayed too close to the flock."

Right, and they can't have that. Nobody can know what the flock is doing. That alone makes me dangerous to them.

Although, even if every single person in that damn cult or whatever the hell it is told me this was all about keeping them safe, I would still tell them they were full of shit. This is vengeance. We got in the way of Rebecca's plans. We complicated things. She wants revenge, and she's going to start with me because I was stupid enough to practically hand myself over to her. No, I couldn't have known anybody was aware of the cabin, but I should have guessed. I can't put anything past these people. I need to be smarter.

Though if nobody finds me, I guess there's really no point in getting smarter since I doubt they'll let me live for long. Long enough to make me regret ever stepping foot on the compound, for sure, but then? Who's to say?

Our progress slows, but my pulse doubles in speed. There are voices outside the van now, plenty of them. People standing around, curious about what is happening, who's being brought in. We've arrived. We're at the compound, getting closer to Rebecca all the time. This is it.

"You better hope she's feeling merciful," the driver warns while his friend laughs. "Though I doubt it. She doesn't like being inconvenienced, and you have been a big inconvenience for all of us."

What, am I supposed to apologize? I can barely bite back a remark. Why waste the energy? All they'd do is turn things around on me anyway and make a joke out of me.

It's only when we come to a stop that true panic starts seeping into my blood. No matter how I try, I can't help my panicky breathing—short, sharp breaths, barely enough to keep me conscious. There's no hope of running for it, even if they untied my ankles. They'd catch me before I got more than a couple of hundred feet away. They might even make a game out of it.

I won't give them the satisfaction of humiliating me. But what's the alternative? Rolling over and playing dead? That's basically what I'm doing when my captors open the door at the back of the van, so blinding floodlights illuminate the space and make me wince, squeezing my eyes shut against it.

"Don't even think about trying any of your tricks." Now

that we're face-to-face, I see the driver and the scar running from over his right eye down the side of his face. It's not easy to look at, but I force myself to do it, staring at him in silence. What did he do to earn that?

"She still thinks she's getting out of this," his friend predicts. They're both laughing as they drag me from the van, letting me drop onto the ground with no way of bracing myself or catching my fall. I land hard enough to knock the breath out of my lungs, and there's one wild, terrified moment where I'm afraid I won't be able to breathe again, where I can't suck in any air. I can only gasp while my captors laugh louder than ever. All I can make out is their shadows looming over me, black against a sky so bright it's almost white. I hope I get to see them die. I hope I get to hear their screams before they do.

"What are you waiting for? Bring her to me, now."

Nobody needs to tell me who that sharp voice belongs to. The air I finally manage to pull into my lungs feels icy cold now, but I do my best to be strong as I'm pulled to my feet, then dragged, thanks to the fact that my ankles are still bound. I deliberately let my body sag between the two men, making it more of a chore to move me, but that childish trick doesn't get me very far. Before I know it, I'm deposited at the feet of none other than Rebecca herself.

"Look at you." The toes of her leather shoes—beaten and worn—are only inches from my face before I'm pulled up to my knees by the men standing around us. It's a good thing they moved me when they did, since I wouldn't put it past her to kick me in the face.

"That's right," one of the men mutters. "You should be on your knees in front of her. In front of all of us."

"That will be enough, Joshua." I can't tell if Rebecca sounds tired or bored. "There will be no need for added commentary. This is between me and our guest. I'm sure there are chores you're behind on after your journey."

It feels wrong, the rush of satisfaction that comes from hearing him put in his place. The way he stammers behind me is even better. "Don't you need—"

"I will let you know what I need, and at the moment, I need you to return to your assigned duties. Both of you," she adds, jerking her chin. "Go ahead."

As she speaks, she lowers herself into a crouch, only stopping when we're face-to-face. She's still got that whole *Little House on the Prairie* vibe going on with her clothes and the long braid that dangles over her shoulder.

I'm looking into the face of evil, but I can't look away. I won't let myself do it. The people who lived here, were abused here, and died here didn't get the luxury of looking away. If this is the last thing I ever do, I'll be damned if I end up crying or whimpering or begging for mercy that will never come.

All I can do is stare at her, watching as her thin lips twitch in what might look like a smile if she had a soul. It comes off as more of a grotesque parody, something rotten, chilling. "So. We meet again." She actually manages to sound almost pleasant. "I did so hope we would see each other one last time."

"Do you have any idea who my father is and what he is going to do to you if you put a finger on me?"

"I'm well aware of who your father is and how he tried to bring our little community down before. It is you who doesn't understand the kind of power I hold, my dear."

When I don't respond except to glare at her, she stands and clears her throat. "A few lashes from the whip will loosen you up," she decides. I barely have time to process this before two pairs of hands grab me under my arms and haul me to my feet. I don't even know where they came from. They must have been standing guard by the door. Between the two men, I'm practically carried to one of the longhouses. It doesn't matter that I go dead weight on them. They're too strong and probably too eager to watch me be punished.

They can't be talking about actual whipping. I refuse to believe it.

Turns out, it doesn't matter what I refuse to believe. There's no stopping them from taking me inside, where the windows are covered in cardboard and there's hardly a trace of fresh air. It's stale in here, but what's worse is the underlying stench of blood and piss.

It's when they untie my wrists and force me face-first over a bench that I finally get it. They're not bluffing. Not when one of them wraps leather cuffs around my wrists to hold my arms in place against the bench's underside. "No," I grunt, fighting to get up and failing when a hand in the middle of my back shoves me down.

Then it lifts my hoody, exposing my back. Sheer terror

blooms in my chest and comes out as a throaty scream. "No! Don't do this!"

I'm talking to myself.

And once the whipping begins, once my skin splits and white-hot pain consumes my every thought, my voice finally breaks. Not that it matters.

There's nobody around to hear me who actually cares.

6
REN

I don't understand what happened.

It's been days since I woke up alone in bed at the cabin, with my head pounding. I still don't know why, and the dull ache I can't shake is like a constant reminder of that first horrible moment when I figured out the truth.

She left me. All her talk about wanting to stay with me, the two of us against everybody, it was all lies. I don't want to believe that, but the evidence is kind of in front of my face. I can't ignore it. She didn't even leave a note to explain why she ran off. She just… walked away.

But River wrote a note. River told me all about what they did when I must've been unconscious after whatever caused my head to hurt the way it did. I can't make any sense out of it, but I know his writing.

When I look down at my fists, I understand why I feel pain in my hands. They're clenched so tight my nails are biting into my palms. I don't really care, pain doesn't last forever. At least, my physical pain won't. Even my head hurts a lot less than it did when I first woke up alone in the cabin. There are other kinds of pain that can last a lot longer.

Like knowing the woman you love had sex with your brother.

Like knowing she left you right after.

He always said he knew her better than I did, right? I wouldn't be surprised if he fucked her just to prove a point that she could never be trusted.

This isn't the time for me to think about River, but his warnings won't stop repeating in my head. She doesn't understand us, she's not part of this, she can't help us. I was so sure he was wrong. I would've bet my life on it.

I'm starting to think he was right all along. He saw something in her I didn't. He wasn't stupid enough to fall in love with somebody who would desert him when he needed them the most. Not like me.

I'm not even sure what I'm doing here in Reno. It seemed like the only place to go back when I was totally confused and brokenhearted. Somehow, I have to make something out of this whole fucked-up mess. If I had to lose Scarlet, I need for it to be worthwhile in the big picture.

I guess part of me figured I would either end Rebecca or myself. One or the other.

Now, though? I'm stuck. There's no going back, but I can't find a way to move forward. Because I'm alone. I can't even get River to talk to me. I guess he figures I've betrayed him enough.

There's no way for me to tell him I was wrong. That I haven't lost sight of what matters. Maybe I was a little confused. I might've lost focus, but I'm back. My head's on straight now. I want him to know that. I need him to know that.

But he's done with me just like Scarlet is. Both of them left me when I needed them the most.

I'm disgusted by this cheesy hotel room, even if it's been my refuge while I try to get myself together and figure out my next steps. I wonder how many people just like me have slept here. Maybe they were down on their luck, thinking they finally found the answer to all their problems. Maybe they lost everything they had and didn't know where to turn next.

I fall into that second category, though it's not slot machines to blame for everything I've lost. It's not me, either—not completely. I made my choices, and some of them were the wrong choices, but I didn't start any of this. Neither did River.

But as usual, Rebecca escapes without a scratch on her. She can still practice her evil and call it faith. She can still shame and hurt and even kill others, but she'll call it justice. She might even pretend to be sad about it.

My teeth grind together painfully when I imagine her putting on her fake sadness and regret. Even when I was a kid, I knew there was something wrong with it. There was something cold and empty in her eyes. I knew she didn't mean anything she said—at least, not the nice, loving stuff. It was all an act. And I used to look around and wonder how I could be the only person who understood. I would even wonder if there was something wrong with me.

But I get it now. When you get older, you talk yourself into things. You make excuses for people. And that's when shit gets all muddied up.

I made excuses for Scarlet. I told myself and River that she would understand. Yeah, she was a little hesitant because she had never been part of that world. She had never seen all of that stuff with her own eyes. So, yeah, of course, she would be nervous and skeptical.

River was right. She was never going to understand. Only he understood, and now he's gone, too. I lost both of them.

What is there to live for now? The question echoes in my head as I flop onto the messy bed. I've kept the Do Not Disturb sign on the doorknob, so there hasn't been a maid in here to clean the place up. Not that it really matters. Most of the time I've been sleeping, if I wasn't ordering room service. It's not worth having somebody come in here and disturb my peace.

Besides, it's not like I have anywhere else to go while they do the cleaning. I don't trust the streets now. I know there are still recruiters for New Haven lurking around. There always are, always watching for the next victim. I don't need any of them recognizing me. I'm basically a prisoner—comfortable, fed, but a prisoner.

This is one of those crossroad moments. I feel it. I have a decision to make. I can waste whatever is left of my life in this hotel room with nowhere else to go and no one to turn to, or I can at least take out as many of Rebecca's army as possible before somebody inevitably puts me out of my misery. We didn't come this far or make so many sacrifices for things to end here.

It's not like I have anything else to lose.

Once I make up my mind, my body takes over for me, and I don't have to do much thinking while I get my shit together to leave the hotel once and for all. I'm on a mission, and nothing is going to get in my way. Never again.

It's fully dark by the time I step out into the dry air outside the hotel. I don't have to think about my route to the compound. River and I went through the plans enough that the map is practically etched into my brain. Burned into it the way my need for revenge burned its way into me so long ago, I can't remember exactly when it started.

Scarlet's face flashes in my mind's eye, but I push it out of the way. I can't think about her now, not when there's so much else I need to focus on. Like how this could be the end for me. There is a small part of me that wishes I could talk to my parents one more time, to Luna, but I'm sure Xander and Q will have them all against me by now. They have that power. If you're one of them, on their side, they're the best friend you ever had. If not? They're your worst nightmare. No, I'm more sure than ever this is the only way. I have to end it here, now.

That means driving alone. I'm almost glad it's ending like this. I'm tired of carrying everything around inside. The memories, the ugliness, the loneliness. Even when things were good, and I had Q and my family and all that, there was always something missing. Wrong. I'm too broken—you don't come back from the kind of shit River and I went through without scars. That's all I am. A bunch of scars. River tried to warn me about that, too. He told me nobody would understand. Luna was luckily too young to remember any of it. That's why he was the only person who would ever be on my side through everything, good and bad. And there I was, thinking I knew better.

Whatever happens tonight, I deserve it.

There's a pit of dread in my stomach when I roll up to what's probably the closest I can get to the compound without being discovered. I park behind what's left of the old gas station, not far from the compound, and go the rest of the way on foot. The pressure of two pistols against my back reminds me what this is all about. What the stakes are. I withdraw one of them and keep it close to my side as every step takes me closer to the place we were supposed to take down together, me and River. The lights set up around the compound make the razor wire gleam orange against an inky sky. I keep close to the brush lining the chain-link fence, hiding in the shadows.

Just because I doubt I'll make it out of here alive doesn't mean I'm going to be stupid about penetrating the compound. This has to count. If I'm going, I'm taking as many of them with me as I can—Rebecca included.

I make it a point to stay low once I'm close enough that I could be spotted. There are a few people moving around, but not many at this time of night. Curfew is pretty early, as I remember. Can't let people go around doing their own thing. They might start getting ideas about making their own decisions. A disgusted grin tugs at my lips as I watch a pair of men on patrol. They're both carrying some serious weapons, and the way they keep scanning the area tells me something might be up. Something they're nervous about. They can't know I'm here, so I have no idea what it could be.

Until.

They're not on patrol. I finally figure it out once a door opens, and a small, hooded figure is led outside. A woman. I shouldn't be able to recognize her with her head covered, but I would know her anywhere. Even with the back of her hoody glued to her skin by what looks like dried blood.

She cheated on me with River. Left me without saying a word. She betrayed me in every possible way. Let me down when she was supposed to be the one person I could always turn to.

I know all of that, but it's not enough to keep my chest from going hot all at once. Boiling hot, like my organs turned to lava. Somehow, they found her, and I'm already too late to stop them from hurting her.

The one name that comes to mind is the name of the last person who'd want to hear my voice now, but he's the only one who can help. I can't do it all on my own. There's too many of them, and I've seen their arsenal. I know how dangerous they are.

I can slow things down, though, until the cavalry arrives.

My mind's made up by the time I turn and dart for the front gate, bent at the waist, a pistol in one hand while I fumble for my cell with the other. I hope I don't regret this. He might hate me, but he loves his sister.

Quinton picks up on the first ring. "You have to be fucking kidding me, you piece of shit."

I cut him off before he can say anything else. "Scarlet's in trouble. They took her to the compound. New Haven. I'm going to send you the coordinates. You need to come and get her before it's too late."

"And I should believe you why?" He even laughs like the cocksucker he is. "Like I'd go anywhere just because you said so."

"Where's your sister? She's missing, right? They brought her here. I don't know how. I only have two pistols," I whisper, looking around for signs of being spotted. "But I can hopefully keep them off her for a little while. After that, it's up to you. I'm sending the coordinates now."

After a pause, I add, "Don't let her down."

Then I end the call and text him the compound's coordinates. They're burned into my brain like the map of the surrounding area.

After that, there's nothing to do but get in there and make sure Rebecca has somebody other than Scarlet to worry about.

7
SCARLET

My back aches, my skin is burning like a wildfire, but nothing hurts as much as my heart. It hurts for Ren and all the other kids that had to endure this kind of nightmare every day.

I'm in the cell, with nothing but an old, dirty mattress, and the smelly bucket in the corner to do my business in. All I can hope now is that my father will find me soon. Though the chances are fairly slim without the tracker inside of me.

Pulling my knees up to my chest, I wrap my arms around my legs and let the tears run down my face. No one can see me here, can see how weak I am right now, when I should be strong. My father taught me better than this. I should be trying to find a way out of here, but I just don't have the strength.

Squeezing my eyes shut, I pretend I'm somewhere else. I pretend I'm back in my room at my father's compound, where I'm surrounded by security and nothing can touch me.

Bang. Bang.

My eyes fly open at the sounds of gunshots ringing out. I get up to my feet quickly and run toward the door. I press my ear against the metal, hoping to hear more gunshots signaling my father has found me.

Bang. Bang. Bang.

Three more shots are fired in the distance before it suddenly goes silent for a while.

I keep my ear pressed against the door, not willing to give up hope just yet. I can hear shouting followed by a few more scattered gun shots but then it goes quiet for good. I stay in place for a while longer, but there is nothing but a few shouts here and there. My heart sinks. That's not a good sign. My father would've brought an army and shooting wouldn't stop until they found me.

Defeated, I walk back into the corner and sink down on my mattress, wondering how many people have been held captive in this cell. How many kids have been tortured, whipped until they bled, and then thrown into a cell like they don't matter?

I perk up once more when footsteps approach from outside my cell. I'm equally excited and scared, not knowing if this is a rescue or if I'm getting another whipping. Honestly, I don't know if I can take more.

The lock disengages, and I quickly get back on my feet. The door opens further, and three men appear in the doorway, my heart slams against my ribs as I take in the man in the middle, the man who they throw into the cell with me, before the door shuts again, locking us inside our prison.

"Ren!" I yell, running toward where he is sprawled on the floor. Blood drips from his swollen knuckles as I place my hand over his and help him to roll on his back.

His face is swollen too, blood smeared over his forehead, more blood emerging from a cut right below his eye.

"Ren," I whisper, hoping with everything inside me that he is going to be okay. "Can you hear me?"

His eyes remain closed, but I sigh in relief when his lips start moving. "I hear you, Angel. I'm just resting my eyes for a second."

"Please tell me you're okay. You look like everything is hurting."

"You should see the other guys," he jokes, but I don't feel like laughing. "I'm fine, Angel. Just give me a minute, and I'll be good as new." His eyes blink open slowly, and his gaze finds mine immediately. "Are you okay? Did they hurt you?"

"Not as bad as you are hurt."

His face falls, regret and anger filling his steel-blue eyes. Without saying a word, I know what he is thinking. He wants to make them pay for hurting me; he regrets not being here sooner, and he would give anything to take my pain away.

"How did you know I was here?" I ask after the silence becomes too much.

"I didn't. I came here to kill Rebecca, but then I saw you

from outside the fence, and I changed my plan. I figured if they are busy with me, they'll leave you alone."

"Oh, Ren… I'm so sorry I left." At my words, his face scrunches up as if the mere reminder hurts him. "I swear I can explain. It's not what you think. I love you, but I had to get away to figure things out, to figure out what's wrong with you."

"What do you mean, what's wrong with me? I'm not the one who fucking cheated."

"Wait what?"

"River told me," he spits, anger and disgust lacing his voice. "He told me he fucked you in the shower."

"Oh, Ren, you still don't understand. I don't know how to make you."

"How about the fucking truth?" he spits.

"Ren, River doesn't exist. He isn't real." I don't know how else to tell him. I must sound crazy to him, but he needs to know.

"What the fuck? Of course he is."

"He is real to you, Ren, I get that, but he isn't really alive. River died when you were a boy—"

"You are crazy. Of course, River is real. He is my brother. I can't believe you would even say something like this." With each sentence, the fury behind his words is brewing, and I can tell he is close to losing control. I need to make him understand. He needs to believe me.

"Why have I never met River before? Why has he never been in a room with both of us? Why was the screen black when I caught you talking to him?"

"Stop it!" Ren is full on aggravated now. He stands up suddenly, his injuries completely forgotten and ignored. "You are wrong."

"Ren, I'm sorry. River is all in your head." I get to my feet, close the distance between us, and take his hands into mine. "You have to believe me. Please think about it. Really think."

I stare deep into his eyes. A million emotions reflect back at me. Confusion and denial are at the forefront. Then anger takes hold of him once more. "Shut up! Just shut up with your lies. You all lie!"

In a last-ditch effort, I squeeze his hands, begging with all I have. "Please, Ren. I need you to understand. I need you to realize that you are sick and that you need help. You have to—"

As I look deeply into his eyes, I can see the exact moment the switch is flipped. Ren's confused eyes turn dark as a night without stars. His lips turn into a snarl a second before his hand wraps around my throat. My Ren is gone.

"You should have listened to Ren and kept your mouth shut, *Angel*."

River.

I know without a doubt it's him. If it wasn't for the way his cruel fingers dig into my tender skin, it would be the way he calls me Angel, like he's patronizing me.

His grip tightens, and I wheeze out a plea, "please stop." I reach for his arms, wrapping my fingers around his wrist as he squeezes hard enough to cut off my air supply. With the last air in my lungs, I whisper, "I'm pregnant."

Immediately, his fingers loosen, and shock takes over his

features before he throws back his head and laughs. "You've got to be fucking kidding me. That idiot doesn't know how to use a condom?" He finally lets go of my throat, and I don't miss the chance of taking a step backward.

"You know, don't you?"

"You might want to be a little more specific. I know a lot of things."

"You know that you and Ren are the same person."

"Oh, that little tidbit, yeah, I've always known. Not sure why Ren doesn't see it. I guess he doesn't want to believe that he would do the things I have no problem doing. Remorse is something he has, not me."

"You have to tell him," I beg. "He didn't believe me."

"Why would I do that?" He grins mischievously. "It's better for me if he doesn't know."

"You have to care about Ren. He is part of you."

"I care about no one and no one cares about me." My heart breaks a little at his statement.

"That's not true. I care about you."

River scoffs. "No, you only care about Ren. You hate me."

"I did hate you before, yes," I admit. "But I could never hate you now, knowing that you are part of him." I take a careful step toward him.

His expression suddenly changes, like he can't believe I just said that. It must be hard to believe that anyone could like him. He doesn't move as I close the distance between us until there's only a few inches from my chest to his. I get up on my toes and tilt my head up to his so my lips brush against his.

He is stunned into silence, unmoving with shock at my sudden action. I catch the confusion in his eyes just before I close mine and press my lips to his with a searing kiss. My whole body lights up, butterflies take flight in my stomach, electricity flows between us like this is our first kiss. I guess, in a way, it is.

His lips move against mine, hesitantly, which only makes me lean in further. Lifting my arms, I wrap them around his neck, pulling him closer. His hands find my hips, his thumbs digging into my skin possessively. I moan into his mouth, and I can feel a smirk form on his lips.

For a moment, I feel a connection between us. The same connection I feel with Ren. It crashes into me suddenly, and just as quickly, it disappears.

His hands disappear from my hips before he shoves me away from him. I stare at him, stunned, as his expression turns cruel and distant.

"I don't have time for this. Unless you want to fuck, don't be a tease."

"Don't shove me like that," I threaten.

"Or what?" He catches my bluff. "You gonna shove back? Or you gonna call your big brother to fight me?"

"Maybe I'll stop liking you again."

"Oh no, not that," he mocks sarcastically. "As if I give a shit."

"I think you do. Because I didn't miss the hurt in your voice when you thought I hated you."

He shakes his head. "Whatever makes you sleep better at night, *Angel*," he snaps before turning away from me.

Maybe it is wishful thinking, but maybe, just maybe, I'm right, and River wants me to love him.

8
REN

It's weird. Am I losing time? Blacking out or something? The last thing I remember was fighting with Scarlet. I'm not proud of how easy it was to lose my temper, but if there's anybody in the world who could make me do it, it's her.

So how did I end up here? Stretched out on a filthy, stinking mattress?

At first, I can't remember why I was so pissed—until I do. It all comes back, slamming into me like an express train. Where the hell does she get off telling me there's no River? It has to be something her family put her up to. They won't rest until they have me locked away somewhere.

Just the memory of the bullshit coming out of her mouth makes my body go hot before a sick feeling spreads through me. Like a drop of ink in a glass of water.

That must be why I laid down. She started with that bullshit and made my head hurt. It hurts now and only gets worse the harder I try to concentrate and figure things out. I should be worrying about how to get us out of here and whether Q took me seriously when I called him. For once, I need him to listen to somebody other than himself. I can't believe there was a time I used to laugh at his bullshit.

This filthy mattress barely deserves the name. I'm pretty sure I feel every inch of the ground underneath me as I roll over, looking around in the grimy, dark room. No, it's more like a cell. We're both in prison. It doesn't take long for my eyes to adjust to the darkness, and I can identify Scarlet huddled and shaking in the opposite corner. "Do yourself a favor," I mutter. "Pull the back of your sweat shirt away from your skin if you haven't lately."

"Why would—" She stops herself before finishing the question, probably because she's not dumb. She's just not as used to this kind of thing as I am. This is her first time being held like this. Being beaten and whipped.

She does as she's told, for once. I still don't know how to feel about her or any of the things she said, but that doesn't mean I don't wince when I recognize the way she hisses through her teeth as the material that was stuck to her skin gets pulled free. "Good thinking," she finally whispers once she's finished, shaky but strong. She's always been strong.

"How many times did they hit you?"

Her head snaps up and her eyes seek me out. Once they land on me, she sighs. "I don't know. I lost count. It felt like a hundred, but maybe eight or ten."

"Even one is more than enough."

She nods, groaning, then pulls her knees up to her chest. "How are you feeling now?"

"Like I got the shit kicked out of me. But my head..." I squeeze my eyes shut when the room spins. All I tried to do was sit up, but it's like my body has other ideas. I can barely move. Completely wiped out. How am I supposed to help either of us when I'm like this? Then again, what else is there for me to do?

"Can I ask you something?" Her voice is soft, barely a whisper, and it seems like she's forcing it out. It must be pretty important, so I nod as much as I can with my head pounding. "Do you remember what happened before you went to sleep?"

My teeth grind together before I can help it. "Why would you throw that in my face?"

"I'm not trying to." She sure as hell sounds defensive, though. "I'm asking a simple question. Do you remember?"

"Yeah, I remember you trying to defend yourself by making shit up." A pain in my head takes away anything else I'm about to say. It's like somebody's driving an ice pick into my brain and fishing around. I don't like showing pain—I never have—but I can't help gripping my head in both hands like I'm afraid it will crack open otherwise.

"You're in pain." Dammit, even now, I hear the heavy sympathy in her voice. I don't want to. I don't want to think of her caring, because then that leads to a bunch of questions. How could she care and still do what she did?

"It'll be fine," I tell her, and maybe I'm trying to convince myself. I have to believe it will be better, or else I might totally lose it. I mean, who wants to imagine the rest of their life in agony?

"You can't let yourself get too upset. Your blood pressure goes up and it makes your head hurt worse. Try to stay calm."

Even through the pain, that makes me laugh. "Oh, thanks. I'll stay calm. You just reminded me of the fight we were having and why we were having it, but sure. I'll stay calm."

"I know you don't want to believe me." Fuck, why does she have to sound so patronizing? "But it's true. It was Luke who cleared up the mystery."

"What mystery?"

"What happened to River."

This again. "I told you—" I start with a growl.

"And I told you to stay calm." If I didn't know better, I would think it was Xander in this cell with me. She knows how to snap at a person in the right way and shut their mouth. "Luke confirmed it. I'm sorry, but it's true. River died at Safe Haven. I know he's very real for you, and I'm so sorry for everything you went through, but that doesn't change the truth. You lost your brother in the worst possible way, and… I don't know, your poor mind was trying to make sense out of it. You were so young."

"Don't talk like you know anything about it."

"I know a little bit," she whispers. I hate that. The pity, the way she tries to make it sound like she knows what this is all about just because she got whipped a few times.

"Congratulations. I wish I could say I had a prize for you." I'm finally able to sit up without everything turning on its side, and I settle in with my back to the wall, resting my head against the cool stone. It doesn't help much.

"I only want to help you," Scarlet insists, because she never knows when to leave things alone. "That's all I want. Can you remember what happened earlier? What's the last thing you remember about the fight we were having?"

"I really don't want to talk about it."

"We have to," she insists. Stubborn brat. She hasn't changed. "It's important. I need to know how much you remember."

"I'm pretty sure we were having a conversation sort of like this one."

"So you remember arguing about River?"

"Right." Why is she torturing me? I don't want to think. Thinking hurts too much. Trying to remember is agony. But she won't shut up.

"Do you… remember what I told you?"

"You mean about how I'm sick? Because that's the last thing I remember you saying." I lift my gaze to find her staring at me with wide eyes over the top of her knees. There's something in her expression that taps on my shoulder, trying to get my attention. What if there is something I'm forgetting? Because I don't remember lying down. I don't remember anything between her telling me I need help and when I woke up.

"That's not what I meant," she announces in a sad, shaky voice. "He came back. You became River."

No fucking way. She's trying to gaslight me into believing I'm crazy. There I was, thinking she betrayed me in the worst possible way. I should know by now there's always a lower level for a person to sink to. "This is bullshit."

"That doesn't mean it isn't true. Do you think I have the first clue how to handle this? I'm really scared for you. I want to help you."

"Congratulations," I snort. "You helped me by getting yourself abducted."

"Fine. You think you know everything?" She shakes her head like she's disappointed in me. Like she's the one who has something to be disappointed about. Like she was betrayed. "Then tell me. What happened before you laid down and went to sleep? Do you remember? Do you remember lying down? Do you remember what I told you before you did?"

I want to. I have to prove her wrong. She doesn't know what the hell she's talking about.

But I can't remember. There's a blank space in my memory. One second, we were fighting, and then here I was. What did she tell me? It must've been something important if she thinks I'm going to remember, but no matter how hard I try, I can't come up with anything.

And the trying makes my head hurt worse. So much worse.

"Enough questions," I finally say.

She sighs, sounding as weary as I feel when she speaks next. "You are right. It's not worth getting into another fight over right now. And we should really be talking about how we're going to get out of here, anyway. Can you think of a way? You researched this place. Is there a way out before they come for us?"

I'm glad to have something else to turn my attention to, even if I don't have any answers right away. At least the room isn't spinning when I stand, then go to the door to listen for anybody on the other side. There are two voices out there, both men, far enough away that I can't make out what they're saying. They sound bored, if anything. Like all of this means nothing, like they're just hanging out until their shift is up. Because in the end, they don't care. They can't care. How else could they live with themselves if they did?

"The best thing we can hope for is to overtake one of them when they come in." Turning to Scarlet, I explain, "We can say you need help or something, and then—"

Even I jump at the gunfire that cuts through the air and kills the peaceful silence outside. Scarlet jumps up with her head swinging back-and-forth as more and more of the rapid-fire shots fill the air. Then there's the shouting—confused orders flying back-and-forth, voices overlapping in panic.

Finally, a siren begins to wail. The compound has been breached.

"What is it, do you think?" It's only when I register the heat from her body that I realize she's standing close to me. I wrap an arm around her shoulders out of habit more than anything else, and I wish it didn't feel so right. I wish I could trust her again.

There are more gunshots, so many more, before I finally realize what we're hearing. "He believed me."

"What? Who?" she asks, raising her voice to be heard over the chaos. "What are you talking about?"

"I called Q. I had to. I gave him our coordinates and told him to get here to help you. I was afraid he didn't believe me."

There are pounding footfalls outside the door, and I pull Scarlet away from it, putting myself between her and whatever's coming. Even if it is Xander and a small army who came through the gate, there's a chance Rebecca comes in here and finishes us off to make sure nobody spills her secrets to the world.

It isn't Rebecca who comes charging through, though. "Scarlet?" Xander grunts. There's a semi-automatic in his right hand, raised like he's ready to fire.

"Dad!" She throws herself at him and regrets it right away, flinching with a gasp when he touches her back.

"What did they do to you?" In the dim light streaming in from outside, it's easier to see what the darkness hid. The ugly blood stains tell a painful story that can't be denied.

"Did you find Rebecca?" I ask Xander as he stares at his daughter's back. At first, I wonder if he heard me; his jaw ticks and his nostrils flare, but he doesn't say a word.

When he does, he sounds like an animal ready to charge. "No. She slipped out of our grasp, but I'm not stopping until she's finished." He tucks the gun into his waistband before taking Scarlet's face between his hands. "What did they do to you?"

Instead of crumbling and sobbing the way most people would after what she's been through, Scarlet stiffens her spine. "I'm stronger than I look. But I would very much like to get out of here."

He shakes off whatever was holding him still and gives her his leather jacket, draping it over her shoulders. "Come on. We're going home."

He pauses, then looks my way over the top of her head. "All of us."

9
REN

I knew better than to think there was any kind of, like, feeling behind Xander getting me out of there. He stormed New Haven to save his daughter. I happened to be there, was all. I'm sure he did it more for my parents and for Luna.

The second we clear the front gate along with the rest of the team Xander brought along, I'm escorted into an SUV while Scarlet is ushered into another. Nobody says a word. It's just understood that I'm not going to ride with them. The most I get out of Q is a dirty look before he climbs into the vehicle with his family.

There's plenty of time to think as we make the long ride back to where I have no idea what's waiting for me. I feel like I should prepare myself for all possibilities, since the last thing I want is to get caught unaware by somebody as dangerous and well-connected as Xander Rossi. My head's still aching enough to be a distraction, but I can't let it get in the way.

They don't trust me. That much I know without anybody throwing it in my face. I mean, the armed men sitting on either side of me in the backseat tell a clear story without a word needing to be spoken. I'm sure Scarlet told her family all the same shit she told me, all that bullshit about River, about me being sick. Why does she have to use that word so much?

They don't trust me, so they will probably keep me locked up somewhere. Either that, or they'll drag me straight to Xander's office and interrogate me for as long as they feel like it. About what? For starters, about all the shit that happened back at Corium. It feels like a lifetime ago.

They won't understand, no matter what I tell them. There's no way. They weren't there. They only think they understand the hell River and I and so many others went through.

What if they want to know where River is? Even if I knew, I wouldn't tell them. I won't desert my brother the way he deserted me. That's not how I operate.

Once we're back at the compound, I'm dragged from the SUV in silence. There's no time to appreciate being back in a familiar place before I'm forced to get moving across the wide lawn. "I can walk on my own," I mutter, not that it matters. They have their orders, and they know better than to slip up.

With both of my arms held in a vise grip, I'm led around to the east wing of the main house while Xander and his kids walk up the front stairs. Scarlet manages to crane her neck and look my way only once, and only for a second, before Xander says something to distract her from me. What is she thinking? How is she feeling? She looked worried, that much is for sure. For herself or for me?

There's a door set in the house's foundation, half covered by ivy. The hinges squeal when one of the guards opens it, and when I peer inside, I see there's nothing beyond it but a set of stairs leading down into inky darkness. There isn't enough room for the three of us to walk side-by-side so one guard stands in front of me and the other behind me, giving me no choice but to descend and face my fate.

The cell they shove me into is small and cold. The kind of cold that seeps into a person's muscles and bones. I've gone from one cell to another. Lucky me.

"Can I get something to drink?" My question goes unanswered. The men walk away on heavy feet, leaving me alone down here with nothing but silence as company. Well, I'm used to being alone.

Iron bars separate me from freedom, though my captivity could be worse. Compared to New Haven, this is a four-star hotel. A sink, a toilet, a cot. Not everybody has a small prison in their basement, complete with plumbing.

I drop to the cot, which is only about a hundred times more comfortable than that shitty excuse for a mattress at New Haven. I might be a prisoner, but I'm afforded a little bit of dignity.

What's the endgame here? Now that I'm locked up, there's the question of what comes next. Why keep me prisoner? What do I need to do to get out? Do they ever plan on letting me out?

New footsteps, and this time they aren't so heavy and plodding. I sit up and face the bars with my hands gripping the mattress. The footsteps get closer. Two pairs.

It's one thing to know Q hates me for everything I've done. I can handle that—I knew this was how it would end up. I followed River's orders because it was more important to get revenge on the man who let Rebecca live than it was to honor my history with the Rossi family. She should've died so all the evil could die with her, but Xander let her slip through his fingers. That much, River and I always agreed on.

It's the way Q is looking at me that's tough to swallow. I don't expect his forgiveness, and I won't ask for it unless I know I'll get it. I'm not going to throw myself at his feet and beg.

Xander clears his throat, standing with his hands folded in front of him. "Thanks to you, we were able to get Scarlet out of there."

"Thanks to you, she was there in the first place," Quinton growls. As if I'm the one who abducted her. Like I touched the whip to her back.

The thought of her back makes me ask, "How is she? I wasn't really able to get a good look at what they did."

That's all it takes for Xander's face to darken while his eyes go hard. "She'll get over the physical pain." I know what he's trying to say without putting it into words. She won't get over the emotional part of it so easily. Or at least that's what he thinks. I know she is much tougher than he believes.

"Somebody kicked the shit out of you," Q observes, smirking as he looks me up and down. He sounds pretty happy about it.

"Yeah. That came after I called you." I touch a hand to my left cheek, where it stings, thanks to a punch somebody gave me back there. Now that I am in full light, the dried blood on my knuckles is an ugly reminder of what happened tonight.

He growls. "It wasn't as much as you deserve."

"Enough," Xander mutters out of the corner of his mouth. "There are other visitors here to see you. I'll give you a minute to wash up there at the sink. I don't want your mother or sister seeing you this way."

Mom. Luna. Shit. As glad as I am to see them, I know what they must be thinking. Obviously, they were already here. They couldn't have shown up this soon after my arrival otherwise. What has Xander told them? How much do they believe?

He's right about one thing. I don't want them seeing me like this. I wash up quickly, not stopping until the water in the sink is clear instead of a murky brownish red. I run my wet hands through my hair, hoping to settle it down a little. By the time I'm finished, there are quick, soft footsteps coming down the hall that runs in front of the cells. I can hear my sister's short, breathless gasp before I see her. She takes hold of the bars, gripping them tight enough for her knuckles to stand out light against her skin.

Before she can say anything, she's cut off. "Luna." Dad's

voice is sharp. I don't know why he's scolding her or whether he thinks I'm dangerous. I only know her face falls before she looks at the floor. Mom and Dad join her, with Dad keeping an arm around Mom's waist. She's leaning against him, one hand on his chest, and her face crumples when our eyes meet.

Now I know what an animal in a zoo feels like. That's how they're staring at me. Like I'm an animal. Like they don't know me, like I'm some predator. An almost sick impulse bubbles up close to the surface, so close it would be easy to give into it. I should give them what they want. I should be the monster they expect me to be.

"Hello," I mutter, sitting on the cot again. Why are they looking at me like that? I know what I've done, yes, but of all people, I would expect them to understand. They know what I came from. Where I was before they took me and Luna in. They know the hell I went through.

"How are you feeling?" Mom whispers. Her chin quivers, but she tightens her jaw like she's fighting off her emotions.

"Oh, I'm in great shape." I flex my right hand, where my knuckles are bruised, if not bloody, anymore.

"We know you didn't mean it." There's a catch in Luna's voice, but what grabs my attention is the way Dad stiffens all at once. When she looks up at him, he shakes his head slightly with his brows drawn together.

"What are you talking about?" I look at them one at a time, searching for answers. It's like we're having two different conversations here, and I don't understand why.

"The things you've done." Dad's voice is tight, stern, but I hear something else in it. Sadness? I guess that makes sense. I'm sure they've heard all about how I betrayed Q and everybody else. This shouldn't come as a surprise.

"I had my reasons." When the three of them stare at me, I shrug. "I don't know what else I'm supposed to say. I did what I had to do."

"Oh, Ren…" Mom turns her head and presses her face against Dad's chest. Her full-body shudder makes my chest go tight.

"And what about… River?" Dad asks.

"We worked together." He winces like he's in pain, making me ask, "Well? You wanted to know. He got out of there, the way I did, and we decided to do what nobody else would. We have to put an end to it, all of it. Don't you understand?" It's so obvious to me.

"You don't remember what happened to him?" Luna's face crumples before she sniffles loudly. "You really don't?"

"Why does everybody keep asking me things like that? Why won't you listen to me?" I feel it happening. The heat, the rage, it wants to claim me. There is nothing more frustrating than trying to defend myself when nobody wants to listen. "Stop looking at me like I'm crazy!" I shout when the three of them do exactly that. They're sorry for me. They might be afraid of me.

Dad's throat works as he swallows hard, then tightens his grip on Mom. "We're going to get you the help you need," he murmurs before putting his other arm around Luna and gently but firmly turning her away from the cell before leading them both away. "We're going to help you."

I can't believe this. How did they all get this idea about me? Why are they so eager to believe it? Like they've already made up their minds.

Why can't I remember what happened after I fought with Scarlet?

No. I don't want to think about that now. My head's pounding again, hard enough to make my stomach churn. I glance toward the toilet, wondering if I'm going to throw up, though I can't remember the last time I ate. How do I not remember that? There's a huge, blank space in my memory. I know I ate at the hotel, but when was the last time I did? I can't even remember what it was that I ate.

I don't want to think about it, but I have to. I have to force myself through it, the pain and the confusion and the questions. The more I try to remember, the more holes I find in my memory. What happened before I woke up at the cabin alone? What happened so many times when I woke up with no memory of going to sleep?

It's like a seed has been planted in me and it's starting to sprout and take root. It grows quickly, spreading through me, filling me with something as close to fear as I've ever known. Not the kind of fear I lived with when I was a kid at Safe Haven. This is the sort of fear that's a lot stronger and deeper, because for once, I'm not afraid of an outsider. Somebody bigger and stronger.

I'm afraid of myself.

What if they're right? What if there's really something wrong with me?

I rack my brain, going back to all the times I talked to

River, all the times I've seen him. I never understood how he got into Corium, how he got in and out without anyone noticing, and until now, I never really questioned it either. Could it really have been all in my head?

Everyone I've ever trusted seems to be so sure River only exists in my mind. Maybe it's time I believe it too.

10
SCARLET

This is killing me. Knowing that Ren is downstairs, locked up in a cell by himself, and my father won't let me see him. I've done pretty much all the begging I can handle; nothing worked. My father won't budge, no matter how many times I ask.

I'm back to pacing my room. I've been walking from one side to the other for so long. I'm surprised there aren't foot tracks in my carpet yet. Running my hand through my too long hair, I think about a plan to see Ren. Maybe I can distract the guard, or I could possibly get my mom to help. I need to do something or I'm going to go crazy.

I'm about to go talk to my mom when the sound of a car approaching the front door has me stopping in my tracks. I walk toward my window quickly to see who is arriving. A silver sedan pulls up right in front of the door and cuts the engine. A moment later, the driver's door opens, and Dr. Stone steps out of the car. Immediately, I perk up. She has to be here for Ren. She is going to talk to him, and I'm going to be there.

Determination flows through my veins as I exit my room and speed walk down the stairs. When I get to the foyer, my dad is already there, greeting Dr. Stone as she steps inside the house.

"I'm coming," I blurt out just as I take the last few steps of the staircase.

My father's head snaps up to where I'm standing. His expression is grim, but his eyes soften when he sees my desperate gaze.

"Scarlet—"

"I'm not taking no for an answer."

"If you would let me finish," my father says, slightly annoyed. "I was going to say you can come as long as I'm there too."

"I'm okay with that," I agree, stunned by my father's sudden change of heart.

Switching my attention to Dr. Stone, I greet her. "Hello, Doctor, I'm glad to see you back." I really am ecstatic. There is still so much I don't know, and I don't understand. I need to know how I can help Ren, and Dr. Stone is the only person who can teach me.

"I'm glad to be back and happy to hear that the patient is present now." There is a genuine excitement in her voice that lets me know she's one of those people who loves her job.

"Please, follow me downstairs," my father offers, waving his hands toward the staircase.

Both Dr. Stone and I tag along behind my dad as he leads

us down the stairs into the long, dark hallway leading to the few holding cells in our basement. With each step, I can feel the tension rising. Dr. Stone straightens her spine, her steps become more hesitant, and her breathing picks up. Her discomfort reaches a new high when we pass the first empty cell. She clutches the front of her shirt nervously.

Dr. Stone clears her throat. "I wasn't aware that the patient is dangerous."

"He isn't," I say before my father can answer.

"Debatable," Dad says under his breath.

We finally get to the cell Ren is being held in. My heart stops when I see him sitting on the cot pushed against the far right wall. He looks up and his eyes find mine in an instant. I suck in a breath, and my heart continues beating in an irregular rhythm. His gaze is tired, his body slumped over. He looks so… defeated.

Stepping closer to the cell, I wrap my fingers around the cold metal bars, keeping me away from the man I love. "Ren," I whisper into the cool, dusty air.

Ren gets up from his cot and takes a step toward me.

"That's close enough," my father warns, and I have to suppress an eye roll. What does he think is going to happen? Ren is going to come through the steel bars and kiss me?

"Hello, Ren, my name is Dr. Stone, and I'm here to evaluate you today."

Ren tears his eyes away from me to look at the doctor. "Hello." His voice is flat, devoid of all emotion. He sounds so hopeless, and it's hurting me more than anyone can imagine.

Dr. Stone turns to my father. "Is this really necessary? I

would like to sit down with my patient and make them comfortable before talking."

"I'm afraid this is non-negotiable. However, I can provide some chairs." He calls for one of the guards to bring three chairs while Ren grabs the back of the cot and pulls it closer to the cell door.

Once the guard brings the chairs, we all sit down, including Ren.

When we are all settled, Dr. Stone gets out her notepad and pen, placing them on her lap. "Scarlet already told me a lot about you, but I would like to hear your side."

"There is not much to tell. I didn't realize there was something wrong with me until yesterday."

"I don't want you to think about it that way. There is nothing wrong. You are simply different. You experienced some trauma in your early life and that triggered a response. This is not your fault." Dr. Stone continues to explain to Ren the basics of the disorder the same way she explained it to us a few days ago.

I listen to it again, memorizing every little word she says while watching Ren closely. He is still tense, just like the good doctor, but at least he is answering all of Dr. Stone's questions so far.

"So, how exactly does the treatment work?" Ren asks when Dr. Stone is done explaining everything.

"Cognitive behavioral therapy is going to be the most helpful in treating DID. There is no medicine for the disorder itself, only for some of the symptoms. In your case, I recommend we start some antipsychotic medicine along with daily sessions of therapy." Dr. Stone turns her head to look at my father. "Those sessions I will have to be in private with my patient. It's imperative given the situation."

My father agrees reluctantly before asking, "So what will the outcome be? If the treatment works?"

"Every case is different, but the hope is to fade the alternate personalities out and merge them with Ren. As I explained, this disorder is a trauma response. Ren projected all the feelings he didn't want to feel onto River. By dealing with his trauma and accepting all the emotions that come with it, he should be able to transition well, especially with daily sessions."

Hearing her say that lifts another huge weight off my chest. She can help him, and she sounds pretty confident about it. "Is there anything I can do to help the progress?" I ask.

Dr. Stone turns to me. "Just be there for him and be understanding. Having someone close to him that cares for him will help him feel more confident and stabilize him during the process."

I look over to my father. "Did you hear that? It would help him if I could come to visit."

My father remains stoic. "We'll see."

Dr. Stone goes back to looking a little uncomfortable being caught between us. "I think that's it for today, but I'll be happy to come back tomorrow at whatever time works for you." She looks back and forth between Ren and my dad. I guess normally she would schedule a time with her patient and not with his prison guard.

"Same time as today if that works for you?" my father finally offers.

"I'll make room in my schedule." She smiles.

"Do you mind seeing yourself out?" My father questions, but it's more of a command.

Dr. Stone gathers her things and stuffs everything in her leather purse before getting up from her chair. "Of course, I look forward to our session tomorrow," she addresses Ren.

The clicking of her high heels has barely faded away when I start bombarding my father with my request. "I think I should be able to see Ren when I want to. He is no danger to me, especially not behind bars. The doctor said it would be better if he had someone, and who is more suited than me?"

"Luna is here and free to see him anytime."

Ugh, I should have known he'd throw that in my face. "Why do you never trust me with anything? You trust Luna but not me."

"Because every time I look the other way, you do something stupid and put yourself in danger."

I glance over at Ren, who is uncomfortably quiet while listening to my father and me fight. "I know I've made some bad choices and put myself in danger, but I regret nothing. Everyone makes mistakes as they grow up, and you have to let me make mine just like you let Quinton make his. I can't be your little girl forever. I love Ren, and I want to be able to at least see him. That's all I'm asking."

At the mention of love, my father's face scrunches up, as

if the sound of that word pains him. "I'll think about it," Dad finally says.

I let out a breath I didn't realize I was holding. *I'll think about it* is a step better than a no. I smile, knowing my dad well and that he is going soft on me. One talk with my mom, and I could have him swayed.

11
SCARLET

My heart's in my throat as I walk to Dad's office. He wants to see me. I don't know why, but I'm going to bet it has to do with the prisoner still locked away downstairs. I hate thinking of Ren down there, all alone. He's already been alone for so long, locked in his mind. Tortured. The last thing he needs now is to be a prisoner. Physically, as well as mentally. But I know better than to fight, especially when Dad and Q still act like Ren should be grateful he's alive. Like not murdering him makes them heroes or something.

I have to push all of that out of my head before I tap on the door. The only sound that comes from inside is Dad's voice ringing out in response. "Come in." I roll back my shoulders and lift my chin before striding into the room like there's no problem.

"Good morning." Like the good little daughter I am, I walk around his desk and lean down to kiss his cheek.

"How are you feeling today?" I ask. He looks tired as hell. Maybe his conscience is bothering him. I can't imagine how it wouldn't. I know he thinks he's doing what's right for the family, but Ren thought he was doing the right thing, too.

"The kid who tried to murder your brother and your pregnant sister-in-law is still locked in one of the cells downstairs." He gives me a sour look before snickering and rolling his eyes while I try not to react to the mention of pregnancy. "I'm feeling wonderful, in other words."

There's an easy way to fix that. Just let him go. Nope, that wouldn't get me anywhere. I have to bite my tongue hard enough to hurt, but at least I manage to keep my thoughts silent.

"Did you want to see me? Mom said I should visit you this morning." Rather than sit in one of the chairs arranged close to the desk, I plop my ass on the corner and fold my hands in my lap.

"Yes, I thought we should talk. There are a few things I would like to clear up between us." He sits up a little straighter in his chair, all business.

My heart is hammering, but I play it off, shrugging. "Okay. What's on your mind?"

He narrows his gaze, looking me up and down. "What is this?" He waves a hand in my general direction, cocking his head to the side. "What's the angle?"

"Who says I have an angle?" All that gets me is a smirk, which makes me groan in frustration. I have to bite my tongue again and calm myself down before adding, "I'm trying to be a grown-up. I'm trying to, you know, meet you halfway. That's all."

"I'm impressed you've turned over this new leaf." His smirk doesn't go away, though. If anything, it widens. In other words, he doesn't believe me. "I've come to a decision. A way for us to both get what we want."

"Let's hear it." It's not easy to hide my voracious curiosity, but something tells me I need to. I want to show him I can handle whatever is about to happen without freaking out or losing my temper. I can't afford to make any mistakes if I want to see Ren.

"You are free to visit with Ren whenever you want."

I didn't expect that, and I sure didn't expect it to come out that way. "Really?" I ask once I find my voice. He always has the upper hand. I should know that by now. He'll always find a way to surprise me.

Holding up a finger, he adds, "On one condition."

I knew better than to think there were no strings attached. "What is it?"

"I want to have another tracker implanted in you."

There might as well be a big, glaring spotlight shining on me. Or maybe it's the headlights of an oncoming truck. Either way, I'm a little off-balance, but do my best to recover. "Oh, is that all?" I ask with a shaky laugh.

"I know how you feel about it."

"But you still want me to get it?"

Shrugging, he says, "Those are my terms. You're free to go down and see him. You can spend all of your time with him, if you want. That's up to you. But not unless I know where you are at all times. How many more dangerous situations do you need to get yourself in before you know I'm right about this? I want to be able to trust you, but it isn't only you we're talking about now. And I can't trust him. Not yet. Maybe not ever, after what he's done."

It hurts to hear it, but I can't pretend like I don't relate. "He needs help," I remind Dad.

"And he's getting it. But he isn't cured yet. There's no telling how long it will be before that happens." He presses his lips together in a firm line while his jaw ticks. I know what he's thinking. He just doesn't want to say it out loud. If it ever happens. There's no guarantee the treatment is going to work, or that he won't struggle with this for the rest of his life. There's no magic pill or potion that will heal him, just like there's no magic spell that will erase the past and instantly rebuild the broken trust.

There's one thing I know for sure, way down deep in my heart. "I can help him. I know how that sounds, but I believe it."

"I can't say you're wrong because I don't know that you are," he admits before scrubbing both hands over his face. This has taken a toll on him. "If you're going to help him, that means spending time with him. Which means you have the tracker implanted."

He's not going to let this go. I guess if I were in his place, I wouldn't let it go, either. Besides, I did tell myself I would always listen to him from now on if I made it out of that compound, and here I am. You don't forget an experience like that. Knowing they were going to hurt me, knowing nobody had the first idea where I was. If it hadn't been for Ren showing up, I would still be there. Whether or not I'd be alive is another story.

Dad is still looking at me expectantly. "Well?" he prompts, snapping me back to the present. "Do I have your consent? Will you allow the tracker to be implanted?"

That's the thing. That's all I'm looking for. The opportunity to consent. He might be backing me into a corner here—I don't exactly have a choice. But I could say no and face the consequences. Right now, I don't care about the consequences. I just want to see Ren.

"Yes. Let's do it." Because it's already been too long since I've had a few moments with him, and it's breaking my heart to imagine him all alone.

A look of relief takes a few years off his face. "I thought you would be reasonable. You'll be glad to know I've already prepared." He pulls out his phone and types a quick message while continuing, "We'll have this taken care of in a few minutes."

"Right now?"

"I didn't think you would want to wait," he says before glancing up from his device. "And I know I'll sleep much better once it's in there, and we know it's working." The disapproval in his voice makes me cringe, but there's no time to explain myself before the door opens and a stranger walks in, escorted by one of the guards.

The next thing I know, I'm led to a chair and asked to pull the top of my shirt down so the doctor—at least, that's what I assume he is—can access my shoulder. "I'm going to give you a little something to numb the area," he explains after swabbing me with alcohol. Dad turns away, staring out the window with his hands clasped behind his back. Funny how a man like him who has shed more blood than I even want to know about can't stand watching something like this.

I suck in a breath when there's pressure. Not pain, but it feels weird just the same. No wonder they wanted me unconscious when they did this the first time. How else could they have implanted it without me knowing?

"All done." The entire process took less than a minute. Now there is gauze taped over the small wound, and he explains how to keep everything clean and dry until it heals. "It shouldn't take more than a day or two, but be sure to let somebody know if you feel heat or pain at the site."

"Thank you." Even with whatever he injected into my muscle, there is definite soreness that wasn't there when I first came into the room.

It doesn't matter. It's ironic, feeling freer than I have in a long time, even with a tracking device implanted in my body. Dad tests it on his phone, and I watch relief wash over his face when it works. I really had him worried.

"Can I go downstairs now?" I'm practically jumping out of my skin. I'm so eager to see Ren.

"Those were the terms. Whenever you please." He doesn't have to like it, though, and he clearly doesn't. But I held up my end of the bargain.

Not wanting to leave without a thank you, I walk back around the desk and give my father a quick hug. He wraps his arms around me and squeezes gently.

Once he releases me, I can't move fast enough, almost running from the room and jogging down the hall. I'm coming. I didn't abandon you.

"Scarlet?" Mom is on her way down the stairs when I cross through the entry hall. "Did you see your father? Is everything all right?"

How did it take me so long to put it all together? "Thank you." Once she reaches the bottom of the stairs, I throw my arms around her.

She laughs in confusion before asking, "What did I do? What's this for?"

"I know you must've talked to him. He would never have agreed to let me see Ren if you didn't push him for a decision."

She pulls back and tucks hair behind my ears before taking my chin in her hand. "Sometimes, our men need a little prodding," she whispers. "Now go. Don't let me stop you."

I would swear my feet have wings, helping me fly to the door leading down to the underground cells. It doesn't hit me until halfway down the steps that maybe I should've brought him something—a snack, a book. Maybe it's better that I didn't since I don't know if I'm allowed to do that yet. I just earned a little bit of freedom, and I don't want to lose it by breaking rules I didn't know existed.

It will have to be enough to reach Ren's cell and be close to him again. And it is. It's enough to make my heart swell until I'm pretty sure it's going to explode from my chest. The way his eyes light up when he sees me, the way he wastes no time getting up from the cot and hurrying to the bars to cover my hands with his.

This is Ren. My Ren. He's back… but for how long?

Stop thinking about that. At least my smile is genuine, because I'm relieved, so happy to finally have a little time alone with him.

"Where are your bodyguards?" he asks with a snicker, craning his neck to look down the hall.

"I don't have any. I can come down here whenever I want now. I made a deal with Dad," I whisper. I don't care about any of that right now. Not when he's touching my hands. It feels so right. I've missed it so much.

His eyes darken. "What did you have to promise him?"

"Doesn't matter," I insist. "Another tracker. I don't care," I add when his face turns to stone. No, the last thing I need is to bring River back right now. Or ever again, for that matter. "Really. Besides, I could've used it when they took me to that awful place. If it hadn't been for you showing up when you did…" I can't go on. I don't need to, either.

His shoulders sink as he sighs. "I did this to you. It's my fault."

"It was my decision," I remind him in a firm voice. When he looks at the floor, I squeeze his hands. "Look at me. I make my own choices—you should know that better than anybody. I could've said no. I didn't. Because you're more important. I have to be with you."

"Oh, Angel…" He touches his forehead to the cool iron and closes his eyes. "I don't know what I did to deserve you."

"Deserve doesn't have anything to do with it. You're stuck

with me." It's good to smile a little bit. "And you're not going to be able to get rid of me anytime soon. I'm going to come down here every day to see you. How are you feeling?"

"Surprisingly good." His eyes are clear and bright again when he opens them. "The doctor came in earlier. She said I had a good session."

"That's great!"

"Don't get your hopes up too far just yet." When I frown, he explains, "It could take a long time. I mean, whatever is wrong with me was there for a long time. It was there before I even knew it was. You can't just, you know, snap your fingers and make something like this go away."

"I'm not an idiot. I know this isn't going to go away overnight. But I'm not going to stop loving you overnight, either." And I'm not going to stop loving our baby, even if I know it's not the right time to break the news. When will that time come? I have no idea. I only know it's not yet.

"Don't give up on me, Angel," Ren whispers, and I have never wished so much in my whole life that I could touch somebody. Hold them. Let them hold me.

I have to settle for looking into his eyes and squeezing his hands tight as I whisper back. "Never. I never will."

12
REN

"How are you feeling today, Ren?" Dr. Stone asks through the iron bars before quickly following up with, "It is Ren I'm talking to, right?" She is wearing her usual business casual therapist attire, but her hair is down today instead of up in a bun.

"Yes, it's me," I confirm, as I sit up and get comfortable on my cot. At least as comfortable as I can get.

"To your knowledge, has River made an appearance since you have been here?" She looks around the small holding cell I'm currently in.

"No."

"Interesting," she mumbles with a hint of surprise before writing something down on her notepad.

"You seem stunned by that. How come?"

"You are very intuitive." She smiles, her eyebrows furrowed, as if she is thinking about telling me something. "Well, if I'm being honest, from the little I know, it seems that River appears in stressful situations and to most people, being confined in a cell would be a triggering circumstance."

Now it's my turn to smile. "Believe it or not, this is the most relaxed I've been for a very long time." I get this is hard to understand for normal people, but I'm not normal. "Before Xander found me, I was on the run… from him. Now that I'm here, and I know he has decided not to kill me, there is no imminent danger."

I wonder if I've said too much, but I also know Xander must pay her enough to keep everything confidential.

Dr. Stone clears her throat before whispering, "Are you not scared he'll still do something to you?" She suddenly looks nervous, as if she is worried she overstepped an invisible boundary.

"If he wanted to hurt me, he would have already done so. He only keeps me in here to keep me away from his daughter. And I don't blame him, knowing what I know now. Until I can control River, I don't want to be anywhere near Scarlet."

"You worry about her?"

"Yes. River doesn't like her, and I'm worried he will hurt her."

"Has he hurt her before?"

"Not physically… at least I don't think so."

"And how do you feel about that?"

"At first I was mad at him, but now I have to come to terms with the realization that I am him." I want to talk to Scarlet so bad. I need to know what exactly I said to her when I was River. What did I do to my angel?

"I don't want you to feel guilty about what you do when you are River. You have no control over that part of yourself yet."

"But River is part of me, so if I hurt her, she looked into my eyes when I did. It was me who said hurtful things to her."

"Scarlet doesn't seem to hold it against you, and neither should you. There are other, more important parts you need to deal with right now."

Placing my elbows on my knees, I lean forward slightly. "And what would those be?"

"We need to get to the bottom of your trauma. We need to go where everything started."

"That's going to be a problem because I don't remember."

"Tell me what you do remember from your childhood. The time before you were adopted."

I suck in a deep breath as I straighten my spine. This is not something I like to recall. I don't remember much about Safe Haven but what I do remember is not good.

"It was just my sister Luna and I. We didn't have parents. We lived in this compound with people we didn't know. People that didn't care much about us."

"Did they hurt you?"

"Corporal punishment was a daily occurrence, yes." I'll never forget the sharp pain of the belt on my back or the sound the whip made when it split my skin. "I got used to it after a while."

"Just because you are used to something doesn't make it less painful," Dr. Stone says, her voice full of emotions. She feels sorry for me, and I hate it. She should feel sorry for the people I'm going to kill.

I shrug. "I could handle the pain."

She doesn't look convinced. "I would like to do a little exercise with you if you are up for it. Some inner child work, but only if you are comfortable. If you feel like you can't handle it at any time, just let me know, and we'll stop."

"Sure," I agree. "I'll try it."

"Great!" Dr. Stone slaps her hands together in excitement. "Why don't you lie down and get comfortable? Close your eyes and take a few deep breaths."

I do as suggested and lie back on my cot, closing my eyes and sucking in a few calming breaths.

"Now I want you to imagine you are somewhere you feel safe and calm."

My thoughts drift to my parents' house. The first place I felt safe and loved. Unlike Safe Haven, my adopted parents didn't believe in corporal punishment. They never raised their hand to us. I didn't have to protect Luna or myself.

"Now I want you to imagine yourself as a child, standing in front of you in that safe place. I want you to imagine yourself before your family adopted you. Whatever age you were when you still lived at the compound and had to endure corporal punishments."

A little boy appears in front of me. Large, fearful eyes yearning for love looking up at me.

"How does he seem? What does he look like?"

"He looks scared, and also a bit angry that no adult is there to love him and keep him safe. He feels… abandoned." I remember the feeling very well. "Alone and frightened, but ready to protect Luna at all costs."

"It sounds like you have always been a protector, first Luna and now Scarlet. That's a lot to take on for one person."

"I can handle it."

"I believe you can, but can that little boy you are looking at? Can he handle it?"

In my mind, the little boy shakes his head. My heart aches for him… for that part of myself. "I don't think so, but he had to." He had to endure way more than any child should.

"If you feel like you can, you could tell that boy that he is not alone anymore. You can tell him it's not his fault and that you understand his pain."

My throat clogs up with emotions. With feelings I don't want to face. I open my eyes and sit up to look around my small cell. Back to reality. "I don't want to do that right now."

"That's okay. You don't have to do anything you are not comfortable with. You did great," she praises me. "This was a good start, and we learned a lot about you already. A lot of useful insights that will make it easier to treat you."

For the rest of our session, we talk about the lighter side of my childhood, good memories with my adoptive parents and Luna, things I don't mind sharing. Quite the opposite, I like to recall them. Those are times I cherish, and I hadn't thought about for a while.

"That was a good session," Dr. Stone exclaims as she gets up from her chair outside my cell. She gathers her things and places everything in her oversized purse. "If you don't mind, I would like to give you a little bit of homework."

"Not sure if I have time. I'm kind of busy sitting around here and doing nothing," I joke, making the doctor laugh.

"Well, if you find a few minutes here and there, I would like you to prepare yourself to talk more about the bad times of your childhood. I know it doesn't feel good, and your instinct is to just not talk about it. But to treat you properly we unfortunately have to go there."

"How exactly do I prepare?" I question.

"Just think about it in your head. We want to be able to validate that little boy's feelings. Tell that part of you that you are stronger now, that you will take on those monsters so he doesn't have to."

"That sounds a little odd, but I guess I'll try it." Not like I have anything better to do.

"Oh, I almost forgot. I brought you a book about DID." She digs in her purse, pulling out a paperback. She hands me the book through the iron bars. I flip it over so I can see the cover and read the title; *Dissociative Identity Disorder for Patients.*

"I will give it a go," I promise as I flip through the colorful pages.

"I'll see you tomorrow," Dr. Stone says before walking down the long hallway. The click clacking of her heels slowly fading away until I'm by myself once again.

13
REN

How do prisoners with a life sentence do this? How do they live day in and day out in a cell, with nothing to do, nowhere to go? Nobody to talk to, either. I swear, if I didn't already have a problem in my brain, I would before long. There's nothing to do but think and stare at the ceiling.

This isn't all about keeping me away from the rest of the family. It's not about keeping Scarlet safe. I'm being punished, too. This is my sentence after everything I've done. It doesn't matter that I don't remember it. It doesn't matter that I could have killed Q, but wasn't able to bring myself to do it. The same is true with Aspen. I couldn't go through with it.

But River could have. River would have. And River is me, and Xander can't forgive that. He might try to help me, but he won't forgive. Which is why I'm isolated, with no entertainment except for a big book the doctor left for me and no trips outside for fresh air.

The only thing I have to look forward to in my day is a visit from Scarlet and my parents, though my family visits are usually short and tense. Scarlet promised to bring dinner tonight, and my heart jumps when her footsteps echo down the hall. "Dinner time!" she calls out. It's the sweetest thing I've heard all day.

I drag the cot over to the bars and sit down in time for her to set the tray down on one of the chairs positioned across from me. There's a slot close to the floor, giving her just enough room to slide a plate underneath. I lift the lid to find a sandwich, chips, a few fresh cookies that smell like chocolate and sugar. I was hoping for something a little more substantial, but I understand the thought process. They don't want me to have anything I would need a knife and fork for. Not yet. Scarlet, meanwhile, has a plate of grilled chicken and roasted potatoes. I'm too hungry to care about the difference right now.

I'm too glad to be with her. Everything is brighter, somehow. Better. It's easy to lose hope while wasting my life away in a cell, but she restores it just by being here. Letting me bask in her light and warmth.

"How are you feeling?" she asks while I take a huge bite of the thick sandwich. It's loaded with turkey and cheese, plus a thick layer of mayonnaise.

"Did you make this?" I ask rather than answer her question right away.

Her head bobs up and down while a pleased little smile

tugs at the corners of her mouth. "I remembered you like it that way."

"I mean it when I call you angel." Taking another bite and swallowing, I tell her, "I'm all right. Bored to death but feeling okay."

"I have to talk to Dad about getting you things to do down here."

"That would be great, but don't push it. I don't want him getting pissed with you because of me." And I don't want him telling her she's not allowed to come down here anymore. She's the only thing keeping me centered now. I can't go through this without her.

"Maybe I'll have Mom talk to him about it," she suggests. "He takes things like that better from her."

She's not going to let it go, so it's pointless to argue. "Good idea." Munching on a chip, I observe her for a while. "How are you feeling?"

"Great. Really, I feel good." So why is her voice so sharp? She's trying too hard. I guess this can't be easy on her, either.

"I would give anything if I could go back and redo everything," I murmur as the usual guilt spreads through my chest. "I hope you know that. I would do anything if I could make that happen."

"I know. But this all started when you were little—-even before you were born. All of that evil… you're not responsible for it."

"I know." I also know she's only telling me what she has to. I know I'm not going to stop feeling like shit for what I did anytime soon.

What am I thinking? I should be focusing on her. Being with her. I have all the time in the world to lie here and blame myself. "What have you been doing lately?"

"Aspen wants me to go shopping with her for the baby." She spears a piece of potato and drags it through some sort of sauce, chewing her lip.

"You don't sound excited about that."

She lifts a shoulder, staring at the plate. "I mean, it's shopping. I like shopping. But it's weird trying to be excited for her when I know you're down here."

"Don't let me hold you back." That's the last thing I want. I've already hurt her enough.

Her head snaps up before her face falls. "No, I don't mean it that way at all. I… I guess I don't know what I mean."

This is probably a good time to talk about something that's been on my mind since I saw the doctor. "Did you ever think about maybe talking to somebody? Like a doctor?"

"A doctor? Why? I'm fine." And she's defensive, too. Why is she so defensive? "I'm totally healthy."

"I mean somebody to talk to about what happened. Back at the compound, the shit I don't remember from the cabin. That had to be a lot for you. Maybe the doctor can help you process it. I want that for you."

At least she doesn't avoid looking at me now, giving me a gentle smile that lights up her face. "That's so sweet of you to worry about me, but honestly, it wasn't all that bad. I'm working through it. And I know that nothing you did when you were River actually came from you."

The way she says it is what gets my attention. That

sounds like something she's told herself a lot. Something she memorized. Is that what she needs to believe? "What did he do?" I ask, voicing the biggest and loudest question, the one that keeps me up at night. "River. I've been lying here, beating the shit out of myself, imagining the kind of shit that makes my stomach turn. And I'm afraid even that isn't anywhere close to what you went through."

"Honestly, he didn't do that much to me. I mean, sometimes you would act a little differently, but there's a reason it took me so long to figure out there was something wrong with you. I just figured you were going through mood swings, something like that." She cuts into her chicken like it's no big deal. I have to wonder how many times that happened. How many times did she have to make excuses for me?

"Anyway," she continues with a sigh, "most of the time, it wasn't so much what he did, but more what he said."

The hair on the back of my neck lifts as I watch her, waiting for a clue to explain what she's hinting at. Finally, I'm tired of waiting. I blurt out, "What did he say to you?"

"It's not important." She's trying like hell to sound lighthearted, but I know better. What, does she think we just met? I know her better than she knows herself.

I watch for a few seconds as she moves food around on her plate. It's an excuse to keep from looking at me. I love her for it, but it irks me a little, too. "I'm not going to break," I mutter, pushing food around on my plate the way she does. "What does that mean?"

Her shoulders rise and fall in a deep breath, which she releases slowly. "It means what I said."

"You don't have to be worried that you're going to hurt my feelings or anything like that. I can handle it. And I should know what… what I've done to you." Damn, that's hard. Part of me knows it wasn't me who hurt her, but I don't want to hide behind that excuse, either. I'm not some pussy who can't face his mistakes.

Clearly, she doesn't agree. Her face goes stormy before she drops the fork on the plate, loud enough for the sound to echo. "Don't say that. Don't you say that."

"I'm not supposed to tell the truth?"

"You didn't do anything! And you know it. Or at least you should by now. Hasn't the doctor told you that?"

"I know what I know." The pain on her face kills me. I'm hurting her all over again. But dammit, I'm not going to sit here and pretend. "I'm not saying any of this to upset you. And I'm not saying it so you'll tell me I'm wrong or anything like that. I'm telling the truth. There might not be a real River, but he's inside me. He's part of my mind. So yeah, I did those things."

"Only because somebody else did even worse things to you when you were too little to handle it. I'm sorry." She sighs when I roll my eyes. "That's just the way it is. I love you, and that's not going to change, and I'm not going to let you punish yourself for something you had no control over."

"Fine. If none of that was my fault, tell me what River did. What did he say? I mean, you're not talking about anything I did, right?" Is it shitty to back her into a corner? Probably. But I need to know. Not knowing is much worse.

"He was mean. He said some really mean things." She spears a piece of chicken and pops it into her mouth, staring at me while she chews. Refusing to look away this time. *There. Is that what you wanted to know?*

"Like what?"

An invisible wall falls between us. I see it in the way her nostrils flare. The light drains from her eyes before she murmurs, "I don't want to talk about this. Besides, it's all in the past now, anyway." I've never seen anybody stab a potato as hard as she does with her fork.

She has a point. Rehashing that shit won't do anything to change it. And if I had half a fucking brain, I wouldn't be dredging it up and forcing her to think about it. "I'm sorry," I offer. Now the sandwich tastes like sawdust, and I'm not hungry for the rest, anyway. But I'd only make her worry if I don't finish the meal, so I force myself through it. In the grand scheme of things, it's the least I can do.

Because I owe her so much more. More than I can ever hope to repay. I could live for a hundred years and not come close to balancing the scales.

Besides, who's to say I won't do worse things to her in the future? There are no guarantees. I don't know if I'm going to get better or whether I'll get worse somehow. What if the doctor unlocks River and the real me never comes back? The worst part is never knowing when it's going to happen. I only know after the fact when it's too late to stop myself.

"You shouldn't come down here anymore." I slide the

plate under the door before standing and replacing the cot in the corner of the cell. "I appreciate it, but it's not safe. I'm not safe."

"What are you talking about? Look at me!" she almost barks when I keep my back to her. "Dammit, Ren. Look at me. At least give me that much."

That's easy for her to say. She doesn't know how hard it is to deny her anything when she's looking at me with those big, innocent eyes.

Eyes that look like they're starting to well up with tears when I gather up the balls to face her. "I'm not going to let you push me away. Fuck that," she mutters, trembling. "I am not deserting you."

"It's not deserting me if I flat out ask you to stay away."

"Well, I'm not doing it. I'm coming down here, and you can't stop me." She picks up my plate and returns it to the tray before adding her own. "Obviously, you're not in the mood to talk, and that's fine. I'll leave you alone."

She's halfway down the hall before she adds, "But I'm coming back tomorrow for breakfast."

Just like her brother. She always has to have the last word.

14
RIVER

*B*lood. There's so much blood. Moments ago, I hoped that the crying would stop, but now the silence is deafening. Now I wish I could hear him cry one more time.

His tiny body is lifeless, his eyes are blank, the spark that was once there gone forever. His mouth is hanging open, blood dripping from the corner of his slack lips. Lips that smiled at me hours ago.

I should've protected him better. I should've done more. This is all my fault...

"Take a good look," a cruel voice taunts. *"You are next."*

I wake up with a jolt. Sweat pearls on my forehead and my heart pounds against my chest heavily. I fist the thin bed sheets beneath me and look around, disoriented. I'm not in the cabin or the hotel, not in New Haven, either. *Where the fuck am I?* It only takes me a few moments to realize I'm in Xander Rossi's holding cell. *Fuck my life.*

Of course, that shithead got us locked up from one cell to the next. Life would be so much easier if Ren would let me take over completely. All of his pesky feelings and need to be a good guy, getting in the way of everything I've worked for.

I get up and walk to the small attached bathroom without a door. I take a quick piss and wash my hands before splashing some ice-cold water in my face. At least I've got plumbing in my cell. There also is a small shelf with a towel and a few changes of clothes. I think I'm getting five-star treatment in this prison.

When I'm fully awake, I walk around the small space, trying to find a way out. It doesn't take me long to realize this cell is state-of-the-art and there is no way out unless I have the key.

Flopping back down on the bed, I lie flat and think about what I'm going to do to get out of here. First, I need to gather some more information. How long have I been here? Why is he keeping me alive? And what is Xander's end goal?

When I hear soft footfalls approaching, I know who it is before I see her. I sit up and look out of my cell through the iron bars. A moment later, she comes into view.

Scarlet is wearing a light blue long sleeve form-fitting dress that goes to right above her knees; her bare legs are pale and soft-looking, and I wonder if they feel as silky as they seem. Her long blonde hair is cascading down her shoulders, so shiny they look like spun gold. In her hands she holds a tray with an array of breakfast foods and two glasses of orange juice.

"Hi," she greets me in her sing-song voice. "Ready for breakfast?"

My stomach growls in response, and I realize she thinks

I'm Ren. I force a smile on my lips. "Of course, I'd love breakfast with you, Angel."

"Great, you came to your senses." She smiles back at me sweetly before placing the tray on one of the chairs outside the cell. She doesn't elaborate on her statement and since I don't know what she's talking about, I simply let it go for now.

She pulls her chair all the way up to the iron bars so I can reach through and grab something while pulling yet another chair up to sit on.

I move my cot closer as well, so we have the illusion of sitting at a table across from each other. Reaching through the iron bars, I grab one of the four croissants and pull it through to my side. I take a bite of the buttery pastry and chew it slowly while watching Scarlet take a sip of orange juice.

"I'm so glad therapy is going well. Dr. Stone says you are responding well. She'll be here in about an hour and a half, so we have time."

Alarm bells go off in my head. They brought in a shrink. *Great.* Ren is trying to get rid of me, of course. I shouldn't be surprised by that or how easily Scarlet is fooled. I can fool the therapist the same and maybe I can get rid of Ren in the process. That would be a fucking plot twist.

"I'll do what I can to fix this," I say with a smile.

"I know." Scarlet's face lights up with happiness and contentment. I hate how beautiful she is when she smiles, but I know she is even prettier when she cries. I wonder if I can make her cry today. Weep for her Ren to come back, or for her daddy to protect her.

"How's your croissant?" I ask as she takes a bite.

"It's delicious," she answers while her cheeks are full of pastry. "Want some jam for yours?" She moves the bowl of strawberry jam closer to me, and my eyes fall onto the small knife right next to it. She must have forgotten that I'm not allowed sharp objects. I could easily grab it and stab Scarlet in the neck. Her bleeding out in front of me, gurgling blood while her sad little eyes look at me in shock.

"I'll have some jam," I say, pushing my thoughts of murder away. Ren would lose his fucking mind, more than he already has, if I hurt her. Could that be the key to get rid of him or would that be the end of both of us? I can't take that risk? Especially now that she is carrying his little spawn. I wonder if she's told him yet. Surely she hasn't told her family or they would have locked her up in her room for good.

I grab the knife through the bars. The cool metal lays heavy in my hand, provoking the beast inside of me once again. Instead of stabbing Scarlet, I use the knife to spread some strawberry jam over the pit of my croissant.

"Did Dr. Stone leave that for you?" Scarlet points at something on the ground.

My gaze follows where she is pointing, and my eyes fall onto a thick textbook lying next to my cot. *Dissociative Identity Disorder for Patients*.

"Oh yes, she gave it to me for homework, I guess."

"Cool, did you start reading it yet?"

"No, but I will today. I was tired last night and went to bed early."

"Are you sleeping all right here? Maybe, I can talk my dad into moving you into one of the guestrooms."

"That would be nice." It would make it ten times easier to break out of this hellhole. "I haven't been sleeping great."

"I'm sorry," genuine concern laces her voice. "I'll talk to him, but I can't promise much. You know what I had to do just to see you." She flinches as if she just caught herself saying more than she meant to.

Curiosity gets the better of me. "What?"

Scarlet sighs, biting into her croissant quickly. She chews slowly, like she is hoping I will forget my question. When I keep looking at her expectantly, she finally gives in.

"I didn't want to bring the tracker up again."

My first impulse is to shrug my shoulders, but then I remember Ren would give a shit. "Oh, yes, that." I play it off like I already knew about it. "I still wish you hadn't done that. You should be free of your father's control."

"It was worth it. I could not stand staying up in my room another day without seeing you."

Another day? Worry fills my gut. How long have I been here and why has Ren been in control for that long?

I won't have answers to those questions now, but at least I can teach Scarlet a lesson and hopefully piss Ren off in the process. Scarlet needs to understand the kind of power I have over her.

Standing up, I move right up to the bars until my body is

pressed to the cool iron. "Come here," I coax. "I wanna kiss you."

Scarlet's full lips pull up in a lopsided grin as she gets up from her chair and closes the distance between us. Her body is so close now I can feel the heat radiating off of her. She brings up her slender hand and weaves it through the bars, cupping my cheek like it belongs there.

I have to fight the instinct not to slap her hand away from me. Instead, I'm leaning into her touch and placing my hand over hers. She pulls me closer, urging my face to meet hers.

Our lips touch, first softly, then with an urgency I didn't expect. My body comes to life, electricity flowing through me like a lightning storm. Her lips move against mine passionately, her tongue softly begging for entry, which I grant happily.

For a moment, I forget where I am, and what I'm doing here, and simply enjoy her closeness. I never enjoy anything; the thought of revenge, pain, and suffering is all I've known... until now.

Scarlet moans softly, pressing her body closer to mine until there is no space between us. My cock is painfully hard, pushing against her warm dress. I want nothing more than to rip that dress off her body and fuck her senseless, but then I remember I'm in a fucking cell, a prison her father put me in, that she put me in.

In an instant, my mind is clear, and I shove the moment of unforeseen happiness away so I can invite the darkness back into my soul.

I move my hand to her wrist where I take a hold of it

before she can pull away. She breaks the kiss with a gasp when I tighten my grip painfully. I weave my other hand through the iron bars to grab a hold of her hip, keeping her in place just where I want her.

"What are you doing?"

"Teaching you a lesson, *Angel*," I taunt.

"River…You won't hurt me," Scarlet says with her chin tipped up like she is confident about her answer.

"You are right, this won't hurt, at least not you."

15
SCARLET

"What do you mean, at least not me?" I question, trying my best to keep my voice even.

"If you behave, this might actually feel good for you."

"What…" My next question dissipates into thin air when his hand moves from my hip to the hem of my skirt and disappears beneath it. His fingers brush against my inner thigh, his rough skin meets my softer one and butterflies take off in my stomach.

I'm frozen, my feet cemented to the ground as he dips his fingers into my panties. I want to tell him to stop, but my throat is clogged up, my mouth dry and my tongue glued to the roof of my mouth. Who am I kidding? I don't want him to stop. Is that so wrong of me? This is still my Ren, no matter what, and I always want him.

His fingers delve into my folds, rubbing over my sensitive clit, making me bite into my lip so I won't moan.

"I was right. You do like this. You like being Ren's angel, but you also like being my little slut."

I squeeze my eyes shut and press my lips together, unwilling to admit that I do like him calling me that. And I definitely like how he is rubbing circles over the small bundle of nerves between my legs.

My pussy grows wetter with each stroke, letting his fingers slide over my sensitive flesh with ease. Shifting my stance, I part my thighs slightly, giving him better access.

"Look at you being my good little whore. Spreading your legs for me like a slut. You like being my sex toy, letting me use you anywhere and anyway I want," River says in a husky voice. This time I can't help but moan, making him chuckle in response.

"Say it… say you like being my slut," he orders as he dips one of his fingers deep inside of me, reaching that special spot that sets my core ablaze.

Shaking my head, I keep my eyes closed, being too much of a coward to look at him while he fingers me.

"Say it or I'll stop," he threatens, and I know he is serious too, already pulling the finger from my pussy.

"I like… I like being your slut," I blurt out, forcing the words past the giant lump in my throat.

"Good girl," he praises. "Now open your eyes and look at me when you come all over my hand."

"Ugh! Please don't make me," I beg. "Please."

River lets go of my wrist, knowing damn well I'm not going anywhere now. With his free hand, he grabs hold of my hair, forcing my head back. His lips are only inches from mine, his minty breath fans over my face.

"Open your eyes," he orders again. This time his voice is a bit sharper.

Not wanting him to stop, I force my eyes open and let my gaze connect with his stormy one. His eyes are filled with lust and a darkness I didn't know I craved until this moment.

"Good slut." A sinister smirk forms on his lips. "Your cunt is so fucking wet for me. If these bars weren't between us, I would fuck you senseless. I would bend you over and fuck you from behind until you scream my name. Tell me, has Ren fucked your ass yet? I bet you would like that too, getting railed in that tight forbidden hole."

I'm not sure what exactly sets me off, his finger pressing against my clit, his intense gaze pinning me, or his dirty talk alone. No matter what the cause, I come suddenly and hard. So hard I have to lean against the iron bars for support.

"Oh, my god." I throw my head back, letting pleasure run through every vein of my body until my muscles are sore and slack.

I am still in a daze of post orgasm happiness when River suddenly shoves me away. I stumble backward, almost falling on my ass in the process. I somehow manage to regain stability. Looking around, disoriented, I realize why he pushed me away.

Down the hall, Dr. Stone is walking in our direction. I glance back at River, who has a big smile plastered on his face. He looks right at me as he brings his glistening fingers to his mouth and wraps his lips around them to suck them clean. I gulp, not understanding why this turns me on so much. Is there something wrong with me?

"Good morning," Dr. Stone greets when she gets closer. "Everything okay? You look a bit… flushed."

"I'm fine," I say, a little too fast and too loud.

Get it together.

I brush my hands down my dress, making sure everything is back in place before I take my seat once more.

"Dr. Stone, meet River," I introduce them like he is a whole new person she's never met.

"River, it's nice to meet you. Would you guys like to finish your breakfast? I can come back in twenty minutes."

"That won't be necessary," River says. "I have nothing to say to you."

"I'm only here to help. There is nothing to worry about."

"You are here to help Ren. I know what you are doing. You are trying to get rid of me."

"That's not true at all. I'm here to give both you and Ren more control, and it starts by having a better understanding of each other."

I'm not sure if she is telling the truth or just saying anything to keep him calm. Either way, I'm not ready to leave. Unless one of them asks me to, I'm staying right here.

"And how is that supposed to work?"

"For starters, I brought you this." She digs in her purse and pulls out a notebook and pen. "I would like you to start writing in it every day, kind of like a diary. You can write about your day, about your feelings, your thoughts, anything you like."

"Sounds fun," River muses sarcastically.

Dr. Stone holds the notebook and pen through the bars, but River doesn't move to take them. She clears her throat and opens the food latch instead to place it inside.

"Would you be comfortable talking about your childhood with me? Ren doesn't seem to remember a lot, and I was hoping you could shed some light on what happened back then."

When River simply stares at me without answering, Dr. Stone continues. "Would you like Scarlet to leave?"

"No, she should stay. I'm sure it would hurt her hearing what Ren and I had to go through," he says with a smirk that makes my skin crawl.

"And why do you want to hurt Scarlet that way?"

River holds my gaze as he talks like he is talking directly to me instead of the doctor. "Because she deserves it. If it wasn't for her, I wouldn't be locked in here. I would have already gotten the revenge I deserve."

Dr. Stone clears her throat and shifts in her seat like she is uncomfortable. "Okay. Scarlet, if you want to stay, feel free, but if you don't want to hear this, you don't have to."

"If she leaves, I won't talk at all," River threatens.

Does he really hate me that much or is he just playing games to mess with me? Probably both.

"I'm staying," I confirm.

"Okay then, let's get started. River, could you share some of your earliest memories with us?"

"Mhhh, let me think." River says, as if he is not taking any of this seriously, but I can see the real pain in his eyes reflecting back at me. "Getting beaten with a belt or a whip comes to mind. Crying myself to sleep is up there too. Not getting fed for days at a time was a fun one too."

"And how did that make you feel?"

"Pissed."

"Anger is a very valid feeling, but usually there is more underneath. Can you tell us what else you were feeling back then?"

For the first time, River averts his vision, looking at something on the ground instead of me. His jaw is tight, and his hands are balled up into fists next to him. Clearly, he's uncomfortable talking about this.

Dr. Stone gives him a few moments to answer, but when he doesn't, she pushes on. "It's easy to be angry, but anger doesn't actually help you heal."

"Who says I want to heal? All I want is revenge."

"And what then? Do you think you won't be angry after? I have some bad news for you. Even if you hurt everyone you feel like deserves it, that dark, empty feeling inside of you will never go away. There is only one way to be happy again, and that is to deal with your trauma."

"I have some bad news for you as well," River tells the doctor. "I like feeling this way. Happiness can go fuck off. You want to know how it made me feel getting abused as a child? I felt weak, helpless, and unloved. But I don't anymore, and I never will feel that way again. I feel nothing but the need to kill, and I won't stop until everyone who hurt me is dead."

"I don't believe you," I blurt out, drawing River's attention to me once more. "You are lying. Everyone wants to be loved and so do you."

River suddenly gets up from his cot, his chest rising and falling rapidly, his nostrils flared. I don't know why me saying this made him so angry, but he clearly is. "Whatever makes you sleep better at night, *Angel*," he finally says through gritted teeth.

"Why don't we change the subject?" Dr. Stone tries to defuse the situation.

"I'm done for today," River announces before turning his back to us. "Thanks for the notepad. I'll be sure to tell Ren all about today." He snickers.

If it wasn't for the doctor, I'd probably take the stupid notepad back.

"I'll walk you out," I offer, and Dr. Stone nods with a gentle smile before gathering her things.

As we make our way to the exit, I can't help but ask, "Are you sure you can help Ren now that you have met River?"

"It will be a long journey, but since Ren is willing to work with me, there is no doubt in my mind I can help in the long run. Just be patient with him. It will take time."

Time. I wish I had enough, but with being pregnant, I've got nine months tops. I need Ren beside me. There is no way I can have this baby on my own.

16
SCARLET

"I'm so glad you decided to come out with me. It's not that I mind shopping when I'm by myself, but it's so much more fun to have somebody to talk to and ask for opinions."

Aspen smiles at me from over the top of a rack of baby clothes. They are adorable, so cute I could cry. Little dresses, little pairs of overalls. The tiniest shoes. My fingers itch with the need to touch everything, to hold it.

To put it in a cart so I can buy it for my baby.

Impossible. I can't even afford to think about it as we move from rack to rack in the cute little store. The mood here is bright and cheerful, and it's infectious. I'm able to smile happily through the jealousy that exists on the edges of my awareness.

I want to be able to do this for myself. I want to be happy about being pregnant. I want to feel hopeful, the way Aspen does. Instead, I carry the secret inside me, knowing it would be a very bad idea to announce it now. At this rate, I don't know when would be a good time to tell everybody. I haven't even gotten up the nerve to tell Ren, mostly because I'm still never sure if River is going to pop out. I don't feel like trying to share a personal moment with somebody who hates me just for existing.

And forget telling my family. I don't even want to think about the horror show that would turn into. Dad would never let me out of my room again. Quinton would never stop bitching and making threats against somebody he was supposed to love like a brother. There's a tiny part of me that wonders if something like a baby would eventually unite us, but I'm not a little girl anymore. I can't afford to believe in the impossible.

"How do you feel?" I'm genuinely curious, and not only because she's my sister-in-law, and she's carrying my little niece or nephew. I sort of want to know what to expect once the months start to pass.

Her eyes cut to the side, where one of the guard's Q insisted on sending with us stands only ten feet away, his back to the front door. There's another guard at the rear exit, as well. Can't be too careful.

She tips her head to the side, and I follow the direction until we are a little further away from any third parties who don't need to hear the details. "Honestly, I feel terrible. I'm tired all the time, and I'm starting to get really big. I might have to get shoes I don't have to tie, since it's getting harder to reach my feet. I'm dreading having to get up at night and pee all the time, too. That should start happening soon."

But even as she says it, it's obvious she's thrilled out of her mind. She went through a lot before this pregnancy came along—she and Q both did. They deserve their happiness.

So why does my heart hurt so bad? Why don't I get to have that same happiness? I want to tear through the store and make up a registry like a woman is doing right now, wandering around with her husband or boyfriend or whoever, aiming her little scanner gun at one thing after another while they glow with joy. I hate them.

"Hey. Are you okay?" Aspen touches a hand to my back, leaning in like she's concerned. "I'm sorry. With everything you're going through, you don't need to hear about my—"

"No, no. Don't even think that," I insist. "I am not going to be one of those people who won't let anybody be happy around them. And Ren is going to get better. It'll be okay."

So why did my voice break just then? Why does it sound so much like I'm going to cry? Hormones, I guess.

"You know, it's all right for you to not be okay," she whispers while her hand moves in circles over my back. "Nobody's going to judge you. You've been so strong. Sometimes, you have to take it easy on yourself and not expect so much after you've been through something difficult."

"I know. You're right. Really, though. I'll be fine."

"Tell that to the tear that just rolled down your cheek." She pulls me in for a hug, which is a little awkward now that she's getting so big, but I appreciate the gesture.

I also feel like a complete asshole for ruining the mood.

Swiping a hand under my eyes, I mumble, "This is supposed to be about you, not me."

She clicks her tongue and rolls her eyes once she lets me go. "Please. I'm not some heartless monster. You're obviously going through it. I want to be here for you."

She does, too. No matter what she's been through, she is always loving and kind. It's easy to see why Quinton fell for her.

Can I trust her? She's never given me any reason not to, but then I've never told her anything this enormous. There are a lot of implications in something like this.

"I have to tell you something." Now my heart is racing and I'm pretty sure I'm going to be sick, but at the same time, I don't want to stop. I want to tell her. I can't go through all of this on my own.

"You can tell me anything." I notice the way she looks around to make sure neither of the guards has gotten any closer.

"I think… I think I might be pregnant, too."

Her eyes fly open wide, and her mouth falls open before she catches herself. "Oh. Wow. Really? That's… great?" She winces, gritting her teeth. "Sorry. I don't know how you feel about it. How do you feel about it? I should've asked you that first."

"It's okay. I'm… I mean, I want to be happy, but…"

"I get it. Believe me." She's chewing her lip and there's concern in her eyes as they search my face. "Your dad and your brother will have some pretty strong feelings about it."

"I know, I know." I roll my eyes and blow out a frustrated sigh. "Which is why I haven't said anything yet."

"How far along are you? Do you know?"

"I really don't. I only know I'm super late. I was late even back at the cabin before I came home. And Ren didn't use protection, so…" I can only shrug since it seems pretty obvious to me.

I can almost hear the plan click together in her head, while a look of determination hardens her features. "Okay. Here's what we're going to do." If anything, I'm glad to hand the reins over to somebody else, so I don't have to be the one thinking about things for once. "We're going to have the driver take us to the pharmacy so you can get a test and make sure. I mean, you need to start taking vitamins and all that. The sooner, the better. We don't want to lose any more time, right?"

Now, I'm so glad I told her. She has the luxury of seeing all of this from the outside, so she can think clearer than I can. "I'm in your hands."

"Leave it to me." Even though we haven't bought anything, she links her arm with mine and leads me out of the store with the guards on our heels. Once we're inside the car, she says, "Take us to the nearest drugstore, please."

He looks at us in the rearview mirror. "That wasn't planned on."

"Well, sometimes lady problems aren't planned on, you know?" Somehow, she manages to keep a straight face while he goes beet red in the mirror before starting the engine.

The closest store is only a few blocks away, as it turns

out. She comes in with me but the bodyguards stand outside —-turns out even big, tough bodyguards don't want to be around when lady problems are mentioned. I would laugh if I had it in me. Right now, I'm a little too nervous. I feel like there's a spotlight on me as we walk down the aisle and come to a stop in front of a shelf full of various tests.

"Which one do I even take?" I can't stop looking around, expecting somebody to discover us.

"Here. This one tells you in plain English whether you're pregnant or not." She thrusts the box into my hands, and we go up to the register, where my legs shake the whole time, and I can barely get through the entire transaction.

"I'm so nervous," I whisper, eyeing the front door, expecting one of the guards to come looking for us. "What if they want to see what I bought?"

Aspen winces, then looks around. "There's a bathroom in the back," she whispers, tugging me in that direction rather than heading for the exit. "Come on. It's only supposed to take three minutes to process."

I can't believe I'm doing this. Sneaking into a public restroom, peeing on a stick, then waiting what feels like forever. Three minutes have never lasted so long. Aspen waits for me outside, and under the door, I can see her shadow passing back and forth as she paces. I always did want a sister. So far, she's pretty much the coolest one I could ever imagine having. No way could I get through this without her.

Finally, once my phone tells me it's been exactly three minutes, I stare at that little wand on the sink like it's going to explode. All I'm doing is confirming what I already know. Why does it feel so monumental?

And why does my heart drop like a rock when the words Not Pregnant greet me once I turn the test over?

Not pregnant. I am not pregnant. How could I have gotten it so wrong?

Why am I crumbling when I ought to be relieved? This is probably the worst possible time to have a baby, for so many reasons. Yet here I am, biting my lip to hold back a sob.

Aspen knocks softly on the door. "Hey. Okay in there? Do you need anything?"

I can think of a lot of things I need. At the top of the list is a shoulder to cry on. I ease the door open, staring at the floor. "I'm not pregnant," I whisper, and just saying the words makes my throat clog up with tears.

"Oh, sweetie." She gathers me against her for another hug, tight and fierce. "I'm so sorry. But, hey, everything happens for a reason. Right? I know that sounds corny, but it's true."

I know she's right. I should be glad, really. We don't need another complication on top of everything else.

But, dammit, I was starting to get used to the idea of having a baby. Mine and Ren's. A part of both of us. The best part, the part that came from love. Now, I have nothing but broken dreams I shouldn't have entertained in the first place. How could I have gotten so far ahead of myself?

"Why am I late then?" I rinse my face at the sink while Aspen waits. If I go out there looking like I just finished crying, somebody at home is going to find out. I don't feel like dealing with a million questions.

"Who knows? These things happen. You've been through so much stress," she points out. In the mirror, I see the way she frowns in sympathy. "Stress can really screw with your cycle, you know? And you were definitely going through plenty of stress. It could be as simple as that."

Of course. My body was busy trying to get through all of the trauma I was experiencing. It's no surprise I skipped a period.

If only that wasn't the case.

If only I hadn't already started loving a baby that never existed.

If only it didn't feel so damn much like I'm losing everything that matters as we walk back to the car and ride home in silence.

17
REN

"Wake up," a deep familiar voice drags me from my restless sleep.

My eyes fly open just in time for me to see a bundle of clothes thrown at my face. I manage to lift my arm just in time, catching the pile of fabric. Still disoriented by sleep, I look around my cell to find Quinton standing inside, only two feet away from my cot.

"Get up and get dressed. You are going to the gym with me," he orders, his tone not leaving any room for a discussion.

I sit up and stare at the pile of clothes in my hand, realizing I'm holding a pair of workout shorts and a thin T-shirt.

"Why are you sleeping in the middle of the day, anyway? Nothing better to do than nap? Oh, wait, you don't," he says sarcastically, glancing around the bare cell with a grin. "Hurry up, I don't have all day."

"Do you really think that's a good idea? Does your father know you are letting me out of here?"

"Don't you worry about him. Besides, you really think you can take me?"

"I know I can take you," I challenge.

"Give it a try and find out, asshole."

A grin tugs on my lips. Fuck, I missed this prick. I know he will never truly forgive me, but Q has been my best friend for most of my life. It's hard not to miss him. Which makes turning him down even harder.

"I don't think it's a good idea to leave my cell."

Quinton rolls his dark eyes at me. "Scarlet and Aspen aren't here. They went shopping, and my dad ordered extra security to follow us around. So get off your lazy ass and put the fucking workout clothes on, or I'll drag you to the gym like this." He points at my jeans, long sleeve shirt, and bare feet.

Only when I look down do I realize he has also brought some sneakers for me.

"Fine," I agree, before quickly getting changed into the stuff he brought.

"Finally." Quinton sighs dramatically as if he has been waiting for hours. "Come on." He opens the ajar door wide and waves me through. "After you."

My first step out of the cell is hesitant and has my stomach in knots. How many days has it been? It feels like weeks. I don't love being locked up in a single room without a window, but I don't hate it as much as I should either.

Like I explained to Dr. Stone, this has been the most

relaxed I've been in a very long time. Being out of the cell has that feeling of safety disappearing while it's replaced with an uneasy feeling in my gut. Having Q walking behind me only adds to my discomfort.

When I hear a second pair of footsteps behind me, my instincts kick in, and I spin around to see where the danger is coming from. A few feet behind Q, one of the guards reaches for his gun, while I have nothing but my fists to protect me.

"Calm down, everyone." Quinton quickly defuses the situation, but I can't shake the feeling of danger.

It's odd because I normally don't fear anything. Quite the opposite. I'm always the first one to run into danger. But this is different because this time the danger is me. I can't trust myself and that means that for the first time in a long time, I'm scared.

"I think it's better I stay in the cell until I have better control of… you know… myself."

I'm not sure if it's my words or whatever Q reads in my expression, but his eyes go wide, like he's in shock before something like pity washes over his face.

"I'm not sure if you're faking it or if you're really that fucked up in the head right now."

"I'm really that fucked up," I answer without missing a beat. "I don't trust myself anymore. What if I try to hurt someone again?" It's probably a mistake to confide in Quinton like this, but I need him to understand that I can't control part of me, and that fucking scares me.

"There's no one here you can hurt. It's just me and you

and a bunch of guards. If it makes you feel better, I won't let you get close to heavy weights at the gym. We'll get on the ring and spar a little bit, and if you go all crazy on me, I'll have the guards kick your ass," he half jokes.

"Aspen and Scarlet are really not here?"

"No. they went shopping for the baby," Q says before cursing under his breath like he didn't mean to tell me about the baby.

"Congrats, by the way. Scarlet told me about Aspen being pregnant. I hope that was okay. Don't be mad at her for telling me."

"It's fine, I guess. Thanks, now can we go to the gym?"

"All right," I agree, shoving my hands awkwardly into the shorts pockets.

Spinning around, I continue walking down the hall, surprised when Quinton falls in step next to me instead of behind.

Together, we walk up the stairs and turn toward the in-house gym. Q wasn't joking when he said Xander upped the security for me because every time we turn into a new hallway, I see a guard standing next to the door, every single one has their eyes on me. If it wasn't for Quinton walking next to me, I would definitely be more nervous with all the attention on me. When we finally get to the gym, two guards follow us inside and position themselves in the corners of the room while two more block the entrance to the gym.

I don't think an actual prison has this much security.

Still feeling a little on edge, I take in the smell of sweat and iron and let it ground me. Quinton grabs two sets of tape and boxing gloves while getting into the small boxing ring on the far-right side of the large gym.

Quinton throws the tape and gloves over to me. We both tape up our hands and put on the boxing gloves; I then climb into the ring, and we get into a fighting position.

I can't count the times Q and I have sparred with each other, but I've never actually been worried about it before. This time is different because I'm pretty sure he actually wants to hurt me, and I'm still banged up from my short stay with Rebecca.

Throwing my hands up to protect my face, I start moving around the ring, letting Quinton throw the first jab. He comes at me with a right hook, but I manage to dodge it. However, his left follow-up jab hits me on the side of my head.

I shake it off and throw my hands up in a protective pose. "You taking it easy on me? I barely felt that," I taunt, and I don't know what in the world is wrong with me. I should be glad he's taking it easy, yet my stupid ego is getting the better of me.

"Don't want Scarlet to be mad at me again."

"Why again?" I question between jabs. "What did you do now?"

"Oh, you know, the usual, being Dad's favorite and getting special treatment, has always driven a wedge between us."

"I always thought Scar was your dad's favorite."

"Not according to Scarlet. She is pissed that I have more freedom than her."

"Well, she is younger, and your parents have sheltered her more than you. She also did not attend Corium like she was supposed to."

"Exactly," Quinton agrees while dodging one of my hits. "She was so adamant about going to MIT, but now she wants to be part of this world that she wanted nothing to do with a year ago. Doesn't she get our father gives me more freedom because I earned it. I've been training for this my whole life while she was reading romance novels and going to frat parties."

"Have you told her that?"

When Quinton doesn't respond right away, I know the answer is no. This is so typical for Q. He always expects other people to read his mind.

"Talk to her. Explain to her like you did me, and she'll understand," I offer. "Is that why you brought me here? To get advice on how to mend things with your sister?"

Both of us are breathing heavy now, sweat dripping down our faces.

"I feel like you know her best… but, no, that's not the reason." Quinton throws a combination of hooks and jabs, one hitting me right in my stomach. "I guess I wanted to see for myself."

"See what for yourself?" I ask when he doesn't elaborate.

"See if you are still the guy I knew or if he is completely gone."

I stop moving. Relaxing my arms, I take in a deep breath.

"I'm here now, but I can't promise that I'll always be myself. I wish I could. I wish I could promise you I'm still that guy and that you can trust me no matter what. But I can't. I can't ask you to trust me when I can't even trust myself. I feel like I belong in the cell, locked away from everybody." This is hard to admit, but it's the truth. I take a step toward Quinton, keeping my voice low enough so only he can hear. "I'm scared, Q. I'm scared out of my fucking mind. What if I try to hurt you again, or Aspen or Scarlet? I can't control River, and that scares the shit out of me."

For a moment, Quinton stares at me like I just grew a second head. He can't believe I just admitted to being scared. Hell, part of me doesn't comprehend it either.

Once he's composed himself again, he drops his fists and sighs deeply. "If you would've just hurt me, I would've already forgiven you. But you… River," he corrects himself, "went after Aspen, and I don't know if I can let that go. For what it's worth, I wish I could help you. And I wish I would've noticed something was wrong sooner."

"It's not your fault," I tell him honestly. I don't blame him or anyone living under this roof.

"I guess it's not really your fault either, but that doesn't change how we feel." I couldn't say it better myself.

No matter what happened or who is at fault, all that matters is how people feel about it now and unfortunately for me, I'm not to be trusted.

18
SCARLET

*D*read makes my legs heavy, but I push through it on my way down to the cells. I promised Ren I would visit, and that's what I'm going to do. If only I knew for sure who I would end up seeing. Is he River this morning? If he is, what do I do? I can't turn my back on him when he needs me, but does that mean I have to put myself in harm's way all the time? River can't do much to hurt me through the bars—that's all I have to go on as I walk down the stairs and into the mostly quiet space. How does he survive down here in all this silence?

The soles of my shoes against the floor make enough noise for him to hear me, and I see his hands wrap around the bars before I'm close enough to make out the rest of him. "Angel. I was starting to think I wouldn't see you today."

I release the breath I was holding. Now my heart beats at a steadier, more normal rhythm as I finish my approach. Yes, he's Ren now, the Ren I know, and I have to bite my lip to hold back the sob of happiness that stirs in my chest. "Sorry, I overslept a little, so I guess they had somebody else bring your breakfast down."

He searches my face. There's a hunger in his eyes. Like he's dying to know everything he's missing while he's locked up down here. "Do you feel okay? Are you sick? You need to take care of yourself. I can't have you falling apart on me, Angel."

"I'm doing my best." I'm also trying to figure out my feelings about the baby, or rather the lack of a baby. How could I have been so dumb? I assumed too much without getting proof. I let myself get caught up in a narrative, and look at me now. Mourning for something that never existed. An idea, that's all it ever was. How sad. The whole damn situation is so sad.

What's even worse is I can't bring myself to get too close to the bars. Just because I came doesn't mean what happened was right or safe in any way. If anybody found out what he did, I would never be allowed back down here, so I can't risk River coming out and doing that to me again. We had a close enough call the first time around.

"What is it?" he asks when I won't come any closer. "Don't I get a kiss?" There's something desperate in his empty laughter, and it breaks my heart.

"I'm just trying to give you a little space," I explain.

"Who says I want space? I've got nothing but space down here." He throws his arms out to the sides. "What I want is you."

Gripping the bars again, he touches his forehead to the

metal and pins me in place with a heavy stare. "What did I do? Tell me."

"You didn't do anything."

Narrowing his eyes, he grunts, "Then what did he do?"

I have to tell him, but I can't dig the words out. I can't make my mouth form them. "He grabbed me," I settle for replying. It's not the whole truth, but I don't know if he could handle the whole truth. What if he gets upset, and River comes back out? At the very least, he'll blame himself, and I don't want that either.

It's not all about him. I don't know if I could admit what he did, because I liked it enough to come—hard. I'm embarrassed and ashamed, and I don't know what any of it means. I only know he couldn't handle it if I told him.

His eyes narrow and his nostrils flare. "What did he do to you?"

I've hardly told him anything, and already he's fighting to keep from freaking out. It's better not to tell him the full truth. "There was no time for anything to happen. Dr. Stone came in for a session." He must buy it, since his grip on the bars loosens a little, and he doesn't look quite so much like he's ready to tear somebody's head off.

Backing away from the bars, he shakes his hands out, growling. "You see? This is what I was talking about. Why can't you ever listen to me?"

"What are you talking about?" I can't let him lose his temper. I need to calm him down, only I don't know how. I don't know what's going on in his head.

"This is why I told you to stay away." Intensity burns in

his eyes until I have to look away. "Now will you listen? What else has to happen for you to figure out I'm not fucking around?"

"I'm not giving up on you."

"That's not what this is about. It's about protecting yourself. From me." He grips the bars again, squeezing them hard enough that his hands go red. "I can't trust myself around you. Don't you get it? I don't know what I'm doing. What do you think that's like for me? Coming out of it, thinking nothing's wrong, and finding out I grabbed you and would have hurt you. It's torture!" His pained cry echoes off the floors and walls, and rings out in my head loudest of all. "I love you. I don't want to hurt you."

"And I know that!"

"But I can't control it yet. I don't know if I'll ever be able to." Slamming his palm against the iron between us, he turns away, cursing and snarling. "You need to go. Stay away this time. I mean it."

"I'm not going to do that!"

"What do I have to say?" He whirls on me, and the look on his face makes me fall back a step. Like an animal in a cage. That's basically what he is, though, isn't it?

"I'll stay away, like this." I gesture between us with one hand, reminding him of the space between my body and his. "I can still come around, but I'll be careful."

"Goddamnit. I don't want you to have to be careful. Do you know how that feels? I can see the wheels turning in your head," he tells me, sounding almost hateful. "Wondering if you're standing too close. If I'm going to go away all of a sudden and leave you with River. It has to be going through your head—don't pretend it isn't. I see it. I feel it. Don't lie to me."

"I'm not lying," I whisper, trembling but standing tall.

"So you're honestly going to stand there and tell me you're not worried at all? Not ever?"

I almost hate him for this. Nobody likes being put on the spot, especially when somebody's glaring at them the way he is glaring at me. Like all of this is my fault somehow. I didn't ask for this. I didn't ask to fall in love with him. I didn't ask for all of the pain in his past, either. "I'm here to help you get through this."

Barking out a laugh, he turns his back on me. "That's not an answer."

"I don't know what you want me to say."

"I want you to say you're taking me seriously," he grunts, pounding his fist against his palm, "and you're going to stay away from now on."

"I can't promise you that."

Slowly, he turns, and somehow the blank expression he's wearing scares me worst of all. Like he feels nothing. Like he's empty, even while looking at me. "I don't want to see you."

"I know that isn't true."

"It is." His eyes go cold and hard as they crawl over my body, but it isn't River staring at me. There's a difference. I feel it. "Stop telling me what's true and what isn't. I know what I'm saying. And I know I want you to go and not come back. Get it? I want you out of here, away from me."

"I can't —"

"I don't give a fuck what you think you can and can't do!" he bellows, and the sound makes me shudder and wrap my arms around myself. "I don't want to see you! Got it? What part of that isn't getting through? Get the fuck out of here and leave me alone!"

He doesn't mean it. I know he doesn't mean it. But how pathetic is it for me to stick around and insist I know what he wants better than he does? Especially when he's looking at me the way he is now, like he hates the sight of me. What if he really does, and I just don't want to face the truth? I guess if a person spends enough time locked in a cell, they can think all kinds of things they wouldn't think otherwise. He might even believe he means it.

I must not move fast enough, since he barks, "What is taking you so long? Now! Get the fuck out of my sight!"

With tears clogging my throat and blurring my vision, I stumble down the hall between the rows of cells. I'm so cold inside, shaking, ashamed of myself for still wanting him the way I do. Even after he used my body, I want him. And I don't know what to do with that feeling. It can't just go away, not something as deep and profound as what we used to share.

I have a single mission by the time I'm on the first floor of the house: getting to my room before anybody sees me and wonders what happened. I don't know if I could handle that. It's one thing for Ren to humiliate me and for his screams to still ring in my ears, but showing anybody how I'm crumbling? I can't handle that.

So, of course, who happens to be walking down the stairs when I reach them? "Scarlet?" Dad takes hold of my arms before I can get past him, and I must look like hell if he sounds this worried. "What happened? Was it Ren? Did he do something to hurt you?"

"Not the way you mean it." I run a hand over my cheek to catch the tears that have spilled over. "He doesn't want to see me. He told me to go and not come back." I know this is what Dad wants, deep inside. Not even that deep, really. It's not like he's made a secret out of wishing I would stay away from Ren.

He pats my arms gently, even a little awkwardly. He's not a touchy-feely kind of guy. "I hate to see you feeling this way, but you must know he's right."

"I knew you would say something like that."

"And you shouldn't be surprised you are my ultimate priority. Your safety matters more than anything. And if Ren is determined to keep you away from him, that tells me he cares just as much about keeping you safe as I do. I'm sure it's for the best, giving him space."

I couldn't disagree more strongly, but what am I supposed to do? Arguing with him would be like arguing with a brick wall. I can only tell him what I know he wants to hear. "Yeah. You're probably right."

"And who knows? After a few days, he could come around, see things differently."

"Who knows?" I echo. I'm only saying the words he wants to hear, but I don't feel them. I don't feel much of anything beyond loneliness and confusion.

When I first hear feet flying down the hall, it's almost a relief. Anything, so long as we can change the subject before I start bawling all over the place. Only when Sophie finds us at the bottom of the stairs and comes running our way, it's obvious something is very wrong.

"Luna," she gasps. "Where is she? Have you seen her? Scarlet, has she called you?"

"No," I tell her. Just in case, I check the phone in my back pocket. There's nothing from her. "What's wrong?"

With a whimper, she turns to Dad. "She insisted on going."

"Going where?" he asks, suspicious.

"Home. She was determined to go home and grab some things for Ren. She took one of the cars—I think Frank was driving," she adds, wringing her hands. "And I can't get a hold of her. They should've been back by now, and she's not answering her phone."

"All right, there could be a logical explanation for this." I hear something else in Dad's voice, though. It's tight, like he's talking through clenched teeth, trying to hold it together for her sake. There is nothing worse than the helpless feeling of watching him calling Frank, seeing his face fall a little at a time with every ring that goes unanswered.

Sophie lets out a broken cry before covering her face with her hands. "I should've gone! I should've gone with her. I should never have let her go alone. Oh, god, what are they doing to her?"

"One thing at a time." Dad pats her shoulder while typing something into his phone with his other hand. "We're going to find her, and we're going to bring her back. This could all be a misunderstanding."

He knows better, and so do I. This isn't a misunderstanding.

It's another shot fired in a war none of us wanted to get into.

This time, it could be Luna who ends up being a casualty.

19
SCARLET

"Don't make me regret bringing you along." Roman looks at me over his shoulder, sitting in the front seat of one of the SUVs in which Dad sent us to look for Luna. "You promised to follow the rules your father set down."

I can still hear Dad's deep voice in my head, and I rattle off the words he used before giving me permission to go with Roman and Sophie and the two extra cars full of armed men. "I promise, I won't do anything to jeopardize anybody, I'll stay close to you and listen to everything you say."

There was no way I wasn't coming along. I couldn't sit around the house, waiting for a phone call. I have to see for myself what happened to Luna. I only hope I don't end up regretting it.

The fact that I would even think something like that makes me grind my teeth. Luna will be fine. God knows Dad sent enough team members along with us in case things get dangerous. I don't think they will. Nobody would ever call me an expert on Rebecca's twisted mind—it's not something I'd be proud of—but I feel like she wouldn't want to stage a fight outside of her own home turf. She would want to feel safe, like she had plenty of people to fall back on.

Or I could be completely wrong, and we could be heading for a bloodbath. The questions running through my head and all the ugly images they bring up make me want to scream until I have to bite down on the inside of my cheek to keep it together. So many what ifs.

Sophie's soft weeping hasn't stopped since she started crying back at the house, and it's enough to break my heart. I feel so damn useless, sitting here with nothing to say, nothing to offer but a soft pat on her arm. "She'll be all right," I whisper, but the words are empty. It's more like wishful thinking than anything else. Something I need to believe, or else I'm going to start crying, too.

"I shouldn't have let her go." She keeps whispering it, almost like a prayer. "I shouldn't have let her out of my sight. What was I thinking? She would've gotten over being mad at me for telling her to stay."

"These people are sick," I whisper. "You can't predict what they're going to do. Believe me." That's not enough to get her to stop blaming herself or to stop the tears from flowing. Like I needed another reason to hate Rebecca. Like she hasn't already ruined so much of what I care about.

There are two SUVs in front of us, and my heart is in my throat as they pull through the front gates with us behind them. Everything looks totally normal so far. What did I expect? There's nothing comforting about the seemingly peaceful atmosphere, though. Goosebumps pebble my arms and the hair on the back of my neck sticks straight up as we draw closer to the house and whatever is waiting inside.

We pull up close to the front courtyard before one of the armed men from the other SUVs hops out and holds both hands up to stop us, glancing over his shoulder at whatever we can't yet see. A handful of guys start up the front stairs, and when I crane my neck, I can see the door is open a crack. Sophie must see it, too, and she releases a strangled whimper.

"I'm going in there," Roman announces. He looks back at the two of us, gripping each other like our lives depend on it. "Stay here. I'll be right back."

"But I have to see!" Sophie insists. He reaches back and touches her cheek before shaking his head firmly.

"It's going to be all right," he insists before getting out and joining the rest of the team. I have never needed to believe something so much in my whole life. Luna doesn't deserve to suffer.

Every second is a lifetime, but it's not long before Roman reappears at the top of the stairs. I recognize the look on his face as he stalks across the courtyard, because I've seen it so many times from the men in my life—my brother, my dad, Ren. He's ready to kill, which tells me he didn't find anything good in the house. But he doesn't look devastated, either, which gives me hope Luna is still alive.

Sophie almost climbs over the seat to get to him as soon as he's opened the door. "Well? What did you find?"

Instead of answering, he thrusts a crumpled piece of paper into her hand. He had it clutched so tightly, I didn't notice he was holding it until now. Her hands tremble as she smooths it out so we can read what's printed in big, block letters.

Ren in exchange for Luna - R

"They killed Frank." Roman's voice is flat, empty. "Shot him in the back of the head. The note was on Luna's bed. That's all we found in there."

Anything else he might have wanted to say is drowned out by Sophie's heartbroken sobs.

REN STARES down at the note while the rest of us watch. I can't stop shivering, rubbing my arms like that will do anything to calm the goosebumps that won't stop prickling my skin. He's too quiet. The sort of quiet that chills me to the bone. What's he thinking?

"I guess we don't need to ask what R stands for," he mutters, breaking the silence. The deep, almost feral anger in his voice makes my heart beat double time. He sounds as close to River as he ever has right now, like he's dangling on the edge between the two personalities. I don't want to set him off—that's the last thing we need, especially with Sophie sniffling in Roman's arms. She can't see that. It would break her after everything she's already been through today.

"We know what we have to do, then." Ren looks at Dad, who draws a deep breath before responding with a nod.

"Wait. What do you have to do?" My head swings back and forth between them. I hate when people have silent conversations in front of me, and the stakes here make it so much worse. "Somebody talk to me, or I'm going to scream."

That's still not enough to get an answer out of anybody. Ren grips the bars, still clutching the note. "Let me out. Let me be part of this."

Now I get it. My insides go all cold and an uneasy feeling creeps up before I blurt out, "You can't! This is a trap!" I look at Dad, desperate for him to back me up, but all I see is resignation in his dark eyes. No, this can't be. "This is her way of getting to Ren, obviously. You can't just walk into that!" It doesn't seem to matter how I shout or how much sense I make. I may as well not be here.

Out of desperation, I grab Dad's arm, squeezing until he looks down at me. "Dad, please. I love Luna, you know I do. But this would be giving Rebecca what she wants. It's too risky."

"The risk doesn't matter," Ren insists. "I don't matter as much as Luna does."

No, no, he can't say that. He can't believe it. This is a nightmare. Somebody needs to wake me up. "But—"

"I can't let her be there for another minute!" Ren is red faced and shaking. "Don't you get that? I'm not letting her suffer. If I have to go and exchange myself for her, that's what I'm doing."

"You know we would never let that happen." Dad's voice is firm, and it has the power to give me a little bit of hope. If he's sure Ren will make it out of this, I can almost believe he will.

"There needs to be a plan," I plead. I look at Roman and Sophie, and they both nod in agreement.

"We know you love your sister," Roman tells him. "But she wouldn't want you risking yourself."

"Of course, we're going to plan this out." Though Dad leaves out the obvious part: there's not much time. He doesn't need to say it. We all feel it weighing on us with every tick of the clock. Ren is practically beside himself, breathing hard, staring at the floor with his hands still wrapped around the iron bars. *Please, hold it together. Please, stay with me.*

"Come on. We'll go upstairs and talk this out." Dad ushers Roman and a weeping Sophie down the hall and upstairs. He only gives me the slightest glance over his shoulder, like he's checking to see if I'll follow. I doubt he's surprised when I stay put. Like I would abandon Ren at a time like this, even for a minute.

"I need to kill her." The intensity of his whispering makes me shiver. He's not even talking about me, but my blood turns to ice, anyway.

"It's going to be okay in the end." Do I believe it? Maybe not, but I need to try. I have to force myself to try. "They're not going to hurt Luna. They need her for a bargaining chip, remember?"

"It doesn't matter. The fact that she's with them at all… it's too much." He scrubs his hands through his hair, growling as he does. "Here I am. There's nothing I can do about it in this fucking cell."

"I know it's hard to believe this right now, things being the way they are… but you know Dad would never leave Luna there. I'm sure they're upstairs putting a plan together as we speak." They'd better be, anyway.

That doesn't make him feel any better. "A plan I'm not allowed to know about."

"Or they're trying not to bombard you." It's useless. He doesn't feel like listening, and besides, I barely believe half of what I'm saying. It's the sort of stuff I need to tell myself to keep calm, or else I won't have a choice but to break down and weep the way Sophie's been doing all this time. It's all I can do to hang on to myself and not completely lose control. Once that happens, I'll spiral when Ren needs me to be strong. I don't want him worrying about me on top of what I know is going through his head about his sister.

"Why did she have to go? Why, goddamnit?" I hate the helplessness in his voice as he slams his palms against the bars between us. "Why did she have to take a risk like that?"

"She was doing it for—" Big mistake. I catch myself before going too far, but not soon enough.

"For me. You can say it." He groans miserably, hanging his head. "She went to the house to get stuff for me. This is my fault."

"Don't even think that." All this time, I've tried to avoid pressuring him too much. Practically walking on tiptoes, afraid to rock the boat in case I end up bringing River to the forefront again. But some things I can't ignore.

"You listen to me," I hiss when he doesn't respond. "You didn't do any of this. None of this is your fault, do you hear me? None of it. You're not the one locking people away. Hurting them, torturing and starving them. That's Rebecca. That's William. That's not you. Rebecca made the choice to watch your parents' house and have Luna kidnapped. You didn't do that."

"You wouldn't understand," he grunts.

"You're right. I don't understand, but I'm trying to. I love Luna, too," I remind him. It's not easy to push my emotions aside and get the words out without letting the tears flow.

"I know you do. Fuck, I don't know what the fuck I'm saying anymore. What is taking so long?" he shouts, looking through the bars and down the hall.

It's not long before the faint sound of a door opening upstairs catches my attention. The door leading down from the first floor. Quick footsteps echo down the hall before I see Q round the bottom of the stairs.

My heart beats a little faster with every step he takes. He won't look at me, keeping his attention focused on the floor for the most part, so I can't see his face long enough to tell what he might be thinking.

When he approaches Ren's cell, I hold my breath. He doesn't say a word. He only slides his hand into his pocket and withdraws a key, which he uses to unlock the door. The squealing of the hinges says more than words ever could.

If only I knew whether Ren was going there to save Luna... or to sacrifice himself in her place.

20
REN

My feet feel heavier than normal as we climb the stairs to get to Xander's office. I look around the house as we walk. This house used to be my sanctuary. Oh, how the world has changed since then. The same halls I used to run down playing with Quinton when we were just boys, now hold guards who reach for their guns when they see me.

"Dad is not going to be happy about this," Scarlet points out the obvious as we approach Xander's office.

"Just let me do the talking," Quinton suggests, and I'm all for it. If anyone can get through to his dad, it's him.

The closer we get to the door, the louder the voices get from inside the room along with my mother's sobbing. Q opens the door and we all step inside.

The room falls silent.

"What the fuck, Quinton?" Xander growls, scolding his son. "What the hell are you thinking?"

"I'm thinking that we need Ren right now and there is no reason he shouldn't help. He already knows Rebecca and her compounds—"

"We can't take the risk," Xander cuts in. "What if he has one of his episodes?"

"River wants the same thing we want right now," Q points out.

"It's true, even if I turn into River now, he would head straight to Rebecca to get Luna. She is his sister too. One of the reasons he told me to get away from you all in the beginning was to keep Luna safe. He wouldn't do anything to hurt her." It's still weird as fuck talking about River like this now that I know he only exists in my head, but it is what it is. I can't change how fucked up I am. At least not right away.

"I know you don't like this," my dad addresses Xander, "But I would feel better if Ren is with us too. Like Quinton says, he knows the place."

"So do I," Scarlet says determinedly.

Quinton, Xander, and I shake our heads at the same time. "You are not coming," Xander tells Scarlet in a stern voice, answering her unspoken question.

Scar frowns and folds her arms in front of her chest but doesn't disagree, even though I know she wants to. She knows there is no way they would let her go with us.

The room falls into a tense silence. My mom is still quietly sobbing. My dad is next to her on edge, and Xander is staring out the window like the answers are about to fly past it.

"Let's just stop thinking about it and just do what we do best," Quinton announces.

"And what's that?" Xander questions.

Q rolls his eyes. "Killing everyone who crosses us," he says, like it's the most obvious thing in the world.

Xander rubs his chin. "He isn't wrong. We are good at that."

If this situation wasn't so serious, I would laugh at the way he is talking about killing people.

Xander suddenly looks at me, his expression stern. "Tell me everything you know about Rebecca and where she could be hiding."

"Since you stormed New Haven to get me and Scarlet out. I'm guessing they have moved to a different location. Rebecca isn't stupid. She probably already had a second location set up. And I think I might know how to find it."

"Please share it with the class," Quinton jokes.

"When I was watching the compound a few months ago, I noticed they would keep carrying stuff into one building, but they never carried it out. It was an unnatural amount of supplies and guns, much too large to hold by the small building, which led me to think there might be a tunnel underneath. That would also explain how Rebecca got away so fast when you came for us."

"A tunnel makes sense. We didn't do a thorough sweep while we were there. After we got you out, we just left but have been keeping tabs on the property, and Rebecca has not returned. However, some people are still living in New Haven and guards have resumed their positions."

"Well, what are we waiting for?" Quinton questions impatiently. "Let's get this show on the road, fuck some people up."

"The main mission here is to get Luna back, unharmed," Roman presses. "Then we can fuck some people up… I mean I'm all about it, but Luna first."

"Agreed." Xander gets up from his chair. "Let me gather a team, we'll gear up and leave as soon as possible."

Scarlet gives her brother and father a hug as they make their way out of the office while my dad holds onto my mom for a few minutes, letting her sob into his chest.

When my dad releases her, she falls into my arms next. She smells like home and my childhood. Warm and safe. I hold her tight as she whispers encouragements into my ear. "You've got this. Just be careful and stay close to your dad. I know you'll find your sister and bring her home. I love you so much."

"I love you too, Mom," I respond before finally letting her go.

Xander, Q, and my dad are already out in the hallway, but Scarlet has been waiting patiently for me in the doorway. As soon as my mom steps aside, Scar closes the distance between us. I hold my arms open, and she falls into them like she belongs wrapped up in my hold. She buries her face in my chest, wrapping her arms around my torso so tightly that I'm surprised by her strength. I lay my chin on the crown of her head, enjoying her silky hair on my skin and the coconut scent of her shampoo.

"I love you," she whispers into my chest.

"I love you too, Angel."

She gives me one more squeeze before releasing me hesitantly. Once she steps away, and I look up, I find Xander standing in the doorway with his arms crossed in front of his chest, giving me what I can only describe as a death stare. Only when Scarlet nudges her dad on the way out of the office does he look away, releasing me from his intense stare.

"Let's go to the armory and gear up," Quinton nods at me, signaling for me to come along. I'm surprised when Xander doesn't interject, half expecting him to put me back in the cell until the moment we're leaving. Instead, I follow them back downstairs to the other side of the basement, where the armory is hidden.

Xander types in a code to the keypad hanging on the wall, a moment later, the heavy metal door unlocks and swings open. I've been inside before, but Xander's stocked up since the last time I was here.

Not only are the walls full of guns and Kevlar clothing, there are also crates with ammo and smaller guns stacked around the room.

"Those new vests are very lightweight and still bulletproof," Xander explains, pointing to some tactical vests hanging on the wall. "There should be enough for all of us. My guys have their own shit in the barracks."

Without another word, we all start to dress in tactical gear, putting the Kevlar on and multiple straps around our waist, legs, and shoulders to hold various sizes of guns and ammo. Once we are all protected and armed to the teeth, we make our way back upstairs and outside, where dozens of black SUVs are already waiting.

We pile in one of the cars silently, while the driver revs the engine and takes off immediately after we close the doors. I took the seat up front while Xander and Quinton are in the second row, and my father is in the third row.

As we drive, we go over the plan of attack in detail. Once again, I tell them everything I know about the compound, which Xander seems quite impressed by.

"You know a lot about this place."

"I spent a lot of time surveilling it," I answer. "I was planning on taking them down by myself, so I needed all the info I could get."

"Did you really think you could go on your own and get out of there alive?" Q question.

"Honestly, for a while, I wasn't that worried about getting out alive. All I wanted was to kill Rebecca." My words make my dad curse under his breath. I know, knowing this must hurt him, and I really hope he doesn't tell Mom or Luna about this. "I didn't care about my own life back then, but that's in the past. I do now."

I know I have people here that care about me and that don't want me to get hurt. Not only my family, but Scarlet too. I can't leave them, and I definitely can't leave her.

It's late in the afternoon by the time we finally roll up to the compound. Before we make it to the gate, Xander gives us all earpieces to stay in contact with each other while we're here. I pop the small device into my ear.

With an army in tow and New Haven's defenses down from the last attack, we don't encounter a lot of resistance. The SUV in front of us crashes into the gate, the already bent metal giving way with ease, letting us drive into the compound.

There are only a few guards present, which are quickly taken down by our guys before we even get out of the SUV. When we do get out of the car, the surrounding area is empty, void of all the people who are usually bustling around.

"Make sure the area is clear while we check out the building with the tunnel," Xander orders his men, before we make our way to said building.

Just as I suspected, we find a latch leading to a tunnel inside.

"We can't wait for backup," I say. "Rebecca must know we're here. If we don't move now, she might be gone."

"Agreed, let's move," Xander responds before telling all his men to follow us through the tunnel via his earpiece.

Guns drawn, we enter the narrow tunnel. It's held up by two by fours and boards on the top, threatening to come down any moment. There is a single string of dim lights illuminating the otherwise dark space, but we can't see far ahead because the tunnel isn't straight. For a while, I fear that this is the trap, and the tunnel will blow up any moment, burying us inside.

It isn't until we turn and find a door at the end that I breathe a little lighter. My father leads the way, with me close behind, while Xander and Quinton are behind us.

When my father reaches for the doorknob, the door doesn't open.

"It's locked," he whispers. "I'm going to kick it in," he warns a moment before lifting his leg and kicking inches away from the doorknob.

The wood gives away with ease, opening up into what looks like a storage room.

"I can't believe they didn't expect us to find this tunnel. This is too easy," Quinton points out.

"I agree. Someone must have warned them by now that we were coming. Where is the welcoming committee?" I question.

"Might be behind door number two," my father points to the only exit the small building has.

"Or they are not here at all," Xander shares his thoughts. "Either way, let's move forward."

My father nods and moves to the next door. Not even checking if it's unlocked, he kicks it open like he did with the last one.

I fully expect the door to lead to the outside. But instead of the afternoon sun, another larger room greets us. Inside, we finally meet the welcome committee.

The first person I see is Rebecca, standing in the center of the small group. Her son, William beside her. Some of her guards surround her, but then there are a few men I don't recognize. And those don't fit in here at all. Dressed in black with tattoos peeking out on their hands and necks. They look more like thugs.

"That's Dimitri Novicov. Russian mob," Xander grits through his teeth, explaining who they are.

We're all holding guns and pointing them at each other but luckily, no one shoots right away.

"Xander, old friend," Dimitri greets in a thick Russian accent. "Glad you could make it. I've been meaning to talk to you about the situation we have on our hands. See, these lovely people here are providing us with young girls for our auctions, so I would really appreciate it if you would not interfere with that."

"They have one of my own, so you bet your fucking ass I'm interfering with that," Xander spits.

"Luna is unharmed and will be returned to you in exchange for Ren, as promised," Rebecca speaks.

"My daughter didn't leave here unharmed and for that, you will pay." Xander raises his gun higher, pointing directly at Rebecca's head. She gulps, her eyes go wide with fear, and I can see her hands shaking from over here. Her son, William, still looking smug as ever. He has no idea who he is dealing with.

I enjoy seeing her frightened, but I also don't want Xander to kill her. I should be the one doing that and no one else.

"I'm sure we can figure someone out that would satisfy you," Dimitri says, voice quivering in fear. "We just got some new young girls in, only fifteen and untouched. You can have one as a retribution."

Xander takes a threatening step toward them. "I want Luna and Ren coming back home with us unharmed, and I want her dead for what she did to my daughter. Agree to my terms or we start shooting."

While Rebecca looks like she's about to throw up, Dimitri simply smiles before he says, "You are outnumbered." His words barely leave his mouth before Xander's men start piling in behind us.

"Are you sure about that?" Now it's Xander's turn to smile.

Dimitri rubs his chin with his free hand, like he is seriously thinking about the offer. Then he looks up at Rebecca mouthing the word Sorry. Shock takes over Rebecca's face as she shakes her head profusely. She opens her mouth to say something, but it's too late. Dimitri lifts his gun to her head and pulls the trigger.

One moment, her eyes plead with him not to kill her, the next they go blank. Her lifeless body crumbles to the floor like a doll. And just like that, she's finally gone.

William stands in shock, starting at his mother's dead body like he can't believe she is gone. His shock quickly turns to anger. Anger directed not at Dimitri, but me. His unhinged gaze finds mine as he lifts his gun toward me. Unlucky for him, I'm faster. I raise my gun and before he has the chance to pull his trigger, I fire my gun.

The bullet hits him in the center of his chest. Blood quickly pulsing out of his wound, soaking his white shirt crimson. He falls onto his knees, still trying to lift his gun higher, but the strength has already left his body. He falls forward, landing on the ground, only a few feet from his mother.

At least I got to kill one of them.

"Go get the girl," Dimitri orders his men, completely unphased with what just happened. "And lower your guns. We're all civil here."

Dimitri's guys lower their guns right away but Rebecca's men stand frozen in shock, staring at their fallen leaders, like lost puppies.

"I said lower your fucking guns," Dimitri snarls, drawing them out of their frightened trance.

Two of the men disappear through the exit. The afternoon sunlight filtering in lets us know that the exit leads to the outside. A few tense moments later, they return with Luna walking in between them. As soon as she sees us, she runs to us, falling into our father's arms. He engulfs her into a bear hug, shielding her from the death inside this room.

"Are we even now?" Dimitri asks.

"For now," Xander responds.

Dimitri nods. His shoulders sag slightly, as if he is relieved not to be on Xander's bad side anymore. And he should be. Xander is not somebody you want to mess with.

Dimitri and his men leave the room while we make our way back through the tunnel. Dad never lets go of Luna, keeping her by his side as we arrive back at New Haven.

My mind is still reeling, trying to let it sink in that Rebecca and William are dead. Even though it wasn't by my hand, she is finally gone. This is what I've been working toward for so long, and now that it has happened, I can't quite process that it's over.

Quinton walks in front of me as we step out into the now

setting sun. Outside, we find the street empty. My father still doesn't let go of Luna, holding her close by his side, as we walk back toward the gate.

I squint against the sun, my eyes not fully adjusting to the bright light yet. I bring my hand up, holding it above my brow to shield me from the sun. That's when I see him perched up on the guard house with a rifle in front of him. A gun that's pointed straight at the person next to me. Quinton.

It feels like everything happens at the same time. The gun going off, me throwing myself against my best friend, the pain radiating through my chest, and then finally me hitting the ground.

21
SCARLET

I can't wait for the cars to pull to a stop before I'm out the door, running down the stairs. I hope everybody knows me well enough to know I couldn't possibly wait a second longer.

All I got was a single text from Quinton: **Everybody safe. Ren injured but OK.**

What the hell is that supposed to mean? Any number of things could've happened. Ren doesn't need to hurt any worse than he already does. When is this ever going to end?

The door to one of the SUVs opens slowly, and the sight of Luna's tear-stained face pulls a grateful sob out of my chest. She looks my way after climbing out and offers a shaky smile that lasts roughly two seconds before she spots Sophie dashing toward her. Seeing her mom is what breaks her, and the two of them weep in each other's arms while Roman wraps them both in a hug.

But where is Ren? I stand on tiptoes, trying to see over the heads of so many men walking around now that they're getting out of the vehicles. Nobody looks like they've been roughed up or anything, so I'm guessing the fight wasn't too gnarly. I'd feel a hell of a lot better if I could get a look at him.

Finally, he climbs out of one of the SUVs followed by Q and Dad. My feet start moving before I tell them to, carrying me to him. I don't care that everybody's watching. I can't help but throw my arms around him after I almost crash into his firm, warm body.

"Easy, Angel," he mutters with a breathless laugh. When I pull back, his teeth are gritted. "I got shot, but the Kevlar kept me in one piece."

He was shot. Somebody shot him. The world starts tilting, and I try to open my mouth to announce I'm going to faint, but nothing comes out. I barely keep myself on my feet.

"That's not the entire story, either." Dad pinches the bridge of his nose when he reaches us, then releases a heavy sigh. "It could have been Quinton. It was supposed to be Quinton. And it would have been, had Ren not gotten in the way at the last moment."

Now I'm really swaying on my feet. My brother walks past, nodding to Ren as he goes. I'm sure he's in a hurry to get to Aspen after a close call like that. At least he gets to be with her. There are no bars separating them.

Thinking of bars clears up the mess in my head long enough for me to realize besides the quick hug in dad's office, this is the first time in ages I've been able to hold Ren with nothing standing between us. And he can hold me. I rest my head against his chest and close my eyes, willing myself to memorize everything—his strong arms, his heartbeat, the sense of security I feel. Even knowing everything I know about him, about how volatile River is and how unpredictable his appearance can be, it doesn't matter. Right now, he's Ren, and he's holding me, and he's alive. I don't need anything else.

"She's dead." Ren's voice cuts through the noise in my head. "Rebecca. She's gone."

I can't stifle a gasp. "Did you…?"

"I wish. But she's gone. That's what matters." He touches his lips to the top of my head before heaving a sigh. Being so close to him, I feel the way he changes. His posture stiffens, his shoulders roll back, and when I look up at him, he's looking at Dad. "Thank you for letting me be a part of that," he grunts, nodding. "I guess I'll head back down to my cell now."

My chest aches at the thought. With my arms still around Ren's waist, I look at Dad, hoping he'll be reasonable. Ren took a bullet for Q. What else does he need to do to prove himself?

Dad must see this, too, because he shakes his head. "No. You can take one of the rooms upstairs instead."

My heart's going to burst. I don't want to show that, though, in case Dad has second thoughts once he sees how excited I am. "Come on," I murmur, letting go of Ren only long enough to take him by the hand. "Is there anything you need? Where did you get hit?"

"My side." He touches a hand to his right ribs, but shakes his head when I make a sympathetic noise. "It's nothing. I mean, it hurt like I got kicked hard when it first happened and it knocked the wind out of me, but it's a hell of a lot better than what would've happened if it wasn't for the vest. Don't worry," he insists.

"Easy for you to say." He's not the one who almost lost the most important person in his world today. If he had died, it would have been for Q. I wonder if this is finally enough to make my brother understand Ren was not acting out of malice when he did what he did. Otherwise, what will it take to make him come around? I don't even want to think about it. It's enough for now that Dad is even letting Ren upstairs. It's progress. I'm going to choose to be happy about that rather than wanting more.

"Are you hungry? Do you want something to eat from the kitchen before we go up?" When our eyes meet, it's like I've finally heard myself. What am I doing, offering him food when this is our first time together with him outside his cell? There are more important things to focus on right now.

It's obvious when his nostrils flare, and he growls softly, that he's thinking the same thing. Instead of going to the kitchen or anywhere else, I lead him up the wide staircase and into the east wing where the guest rooms sit. Choosing one at random, I open the door and find the room already arranged—fresh linens on the king size bed, not a speck of dust anywhere, and the ensuite bathroom will be stocked with clean towels. Mom likes to keep the guest rooms ready for visitors, since there's never any knowing for sure when an unexpected guest will show up. Especially at a time like this, with Roman and Sophie and Luna already staying with us.

It's not them I'm thinking about as Ren steps into the room. I don't care about anybody but the two of us as I close the door behind me and lean against it, breathless and aching, longing to touch him, to prove to myself that he's real. He's alive, they didn't hurt him.

He turns away from the bed to look at me, and all it takes is the briefest eye contact for my body to respond with an intensity that leaves me trembling. But as much as I want to reach out and touch him, I'm frozen in place, overwhelmed by my longing. I could've lost him.

He crosses the room in two long strides, not saying a word before burying his hands in my hair. He crashes against me and covers my mouth before I can make a sound. That's all it takes to unlock everything I've been holding back. All the loneliness, all my need—everything. I pour all of it into him, drinking in his kisses and his touch until I could cry with relief and joy. I'm back where I belong. Pinned against the door with his unyielding body holding me in place, and my ecstatic cries muffled by his mouth. He kisses me deeply, growling as he does, consumed the same way I am. He rolls his hips and drives his hardening dick against me and tears of relief squeeze their way from between my lashes, rolling down my cheeks and wetting his face.

He feels them and breaks the kiss, his eyes darting over my face. "Are you all right?" he whispers, breathing hard.

"Kiss me," I beg, wrapping a hand around the back of his

neck and pulling him down. I'm too greedy for his kiss and his touch to explain. We can talk later. Right now, this is all that matters.

He must agree, since his hands soon begin tugging at the waistband of my leggings. I help him, pulling them down and kicking them off before touching my hands to his waistband and unbuckling his belt. There's no sound but our quick, anxious breaths while we fight to find the relief we both need so desperately. I'm almost sobbing with frustration by the time he drops his pants and shorts to free his dripping cock.

"Quick," I beg, wrapping my arms around his shoulders. "Please. Put it in me. I need you."

He barely takes time to lift my leg and drape it over his hip before skewering me with one sure thrust. The sudden connection makes my body go stiff, my mouth falling open as unspeakable pleasure rolls over me. It's not just physical pleasure, either. I have him here, inside me, where he belongs.

But all it takes is the slightest movement of his hips to leave me burying my face in his neck to muffle my moans. How could I have forgotten how good he feels? "Fuck, Angel." He breathes in my ear as he takes me hard and fast, rattling the door with every deep stroke. "Fuck, so sweet. So wet."

I can only groan, my fingers twisting and tugging his hair as every thrust takes me closer to sweet oblivion. I didn't know how much I needed this, to lose myself in him. All of the hurt and the loneliness and the questions are washed away. There's only us. The way it's supposed to be.

"Getting tighter," he rasps against my ear, his hot breath making me shiver and whimper. My nipples brush against his chest as he moves me up and down, sending delicious shockwaves of sensation straight to my pussy. "Are you going to come for me? Fuck, I need to feel it. I need you to come on my cock, Angel. Can you do that for me?"

Can I? I don't think I have a choice. It's coming on so fast, my whole body tensing in preparation for what I know is going to rock me to my core. "Make me come," I beg, scraping my teeth over his earlobe until he slams into me hard enough that I'm walking the line between pain and pleasure. But I love it. I want him to hurt me, I want him to make me sore enough to feel it after this is over.

"Harder," I beg, then press my face to his neck when he gives me what I want. Harder, faster, until the door bangs on its hinges, and I'm lost in ecstasy. It hits me all at once, like waves crashing against the shore, and all I can do is sob against his skin and cling to him as tightly as I can while he fills me with warmth, groaning against my shoulder and shuddering in release.

"I love you." Just saying the words makes me cry harder. For the first time in forever, though, there's nothing behind my tears except joy. "I love you, Ren."

He lifts his head and looks me in the eye, a tiny smile stirring his lips. "I love you, Angel."

So why do I feel sort of anxious? What am I looking for when I stare into his dark, familiar eyes? I'm looking for

River. Waiting for him to show up and ruin things the way he always does when we're happy together.

There's none of that now. There's only Ren, and I'm grateful for that.

I just wish I didn't always have to wait for the other shoe to drop.

22
REN

A sense of normality sets in as I take my seat at the long dining room table. My parents and Luna sit beside me while Xander sits at the head of the table and his family across from us. My mom is finally back to normal now that Luna was returned to us unharmed. She is smiling brightly at me, the spark in her eyes returned.

Ella also seems unusually happy today, probably because she feels like the family is finally whole again. She's always seen me as a bonus kid, at least that's what she told me many times. I wish I could share their joy without restrain. Unfortunately, there is still so much darkness surrounding me. It's hard to see the light at the end of the tunnel.

Rebecca and William are finally dead, though I still feel like there is unfinished business. New Haven still exists, and though their once leaders are gone, the Russian mob is simply going to appoint someone else to do their bidding. I know it's not my problem, and I shouldn't feel responsible for them, but I also can't just let it go. Young kids are still being picked off the street just like Luna and I were randomly chosen. Those kids are still going through hell every day just to be sold off to the highest bidder when they're grown up.

The maids bring the first course out to the table. A bowl of savory smelling creamy soup is set in front of me. As I reach for my spoon, my father clears his throat.

"Now that Luna is back safely, Sophie and I were thinking about returning to our home. We were also hoping to take Ren with us."

I drop my spoon on the table. That's the first I've heard of it. Shocked, I look over at my father, wondering why he didn't ask me first. I guess he just assumed I'd want to go home. Out of the corner of my eye, I see Scarlet shake her head profusely.

Before Xander has a chance to answer, I blurt out, "I'd rather stay here if that's okay with you." I meet Xander's surprised expression.

"Is that so?" Xander asks, looking between my father and I. "I'm surprised you want to stay."

"Dr. Stone is here, and I doubt she would make the drive out to our house every day."

"I want Ren to stay here as well," Scarlet chimes in, making her father scoff in annoyance.

"Is that the only reason you want to stay?" Quinton questions.

No. Is the short answer. I want to stay because I still want to take down New Haven, and I know I need Xander's help to do so. I also know it's not going to be easy to get his help with this. He won't just start a war with the Russians, without a good reason.

Instead of bringing up my real reason now, I go for another half lie.

"I also want to stay here because it's safer. If I turn into River there are guards and a cell downstairs."

"Or I can just kick your ass," Quinton jokes.

"You can try," I snap back, making us both grin.

"I don't mind you staying," Xander finally announces, though the tone of his voice is hesitant.

Relief washes over me. I wasn't sure if he would be okay with this. Especially not with Scarlet here.

"I'd rather have you home with us, but I understand why you want to stay," Mom explains. "I'll be happy as long as you are happy."

"I think it's a good idea that you are staying," Ella chimes in. "It will be good to have you boys back together. Just don't try to burn the house down again."

"That was one time, Mom." Quinton laughs. "And it was by accident. When will you let that go?"

"When you promise never to try to cook on your own again."

"I swear we'll let the cook prepare all food from now on," Quinton promises, making everyone at the table laugh.

This is nice, a normality I never thought I would experience again. I glance over to my parents and see the same sense of contentment I'm feeling reflecting back at me. Luna smiles at me, she feels it too.

"Have you thought of any baby names yet?" Scarlet asks, her eyes bouncing curiously between Quinton and Aspen.

"We haven't decided yet, but we have a few names on the short list," Aspen explains, excitement filling her voice. "For a girl we like Emma or Emily and for a boy we like Tristan or Briggs."

"Oh, I like all of those names," Ella beams. "When will you find out what you are having?"

"At the next ultrasound in two weeks. I'm so excited. I can't wait." Aspen grins from ear to ear.

I still can't believe Quinton is going to be a father. It's hard to imagine him wanting to be one, but looking at his proud smile now lets me know he is just as excited as Aspen. I guess Q has always been full of surprises. When we first came to Corium, I never thought he would have a girlfriend, let alone a wife. Here he is, happily married with a kid on the way.

The rest of the dinner is spent discussing more baby topics like the upcoming baby shower, the decorating of the nursery, and choosing the safest car seat. None of which I'm particularly interested in, but I enjoy watching all the women's enthusiasm about the addition to the family. A family I didn't feel like I would be part of ever again—until today.

By the time we finish dessert, the sun has set, and my parents are ready to leave to go back home. My mom comes and hugs me first, followed by Luna and my father. After everyone says their goodbyes, Scarlet comes to give me a hug as well.

She brings her mouth to my ear to whisper, "I'm going to take a shower, and I'm going to make myself come while thinking of you."

My cock stirs in my pants at her raunchy confession, and my mind is instantly filled with an image of her fingers stroking her pussy. *Calm down, boy.* I tell my impatient dick.

"Maybe I'll sneak into your room after," Scarlet keeps whispering into my ear seductively. "And I could suck—" I break the hug, knowing if I keep listening to her, I'll definitely walk out of here with a boner. I'm sure Xander will change his mind about me staying rather quickly if he sees me hard after hugging his daughter.

Scarlet giggles before spinning around and exiting the dining room.

I'm about to follow her upstairs when Quinton steps in my way. "Hey, about earlier. I just wanted to say thanks. You didn't have to take a bullet for me, but you did without thinking."

"Don't worry about it," I say, like it was no big deal. "I just didn't want to hear you whine about a bruise all the way home."

"Sure," Quinton slaps me on my shoulder. "Just say you're welcome and move on, asshat."

"You're welcome, prick." I slap his shoulder back.

"I wanted to thank you too," Aspen says, coming up beside us.

"You don't have to thank me," I tell her honestly. She doesn't owe me anything after what I did to her. "If anything, I owe you an apology… for what I did at Corium."

Quinton stiffens at me mentioning the past. He is still not completely over it, and I don't blame him.

"Don't worry about it. It's water under the bridge. But just so you know." Aspen takes a step closer. "If you do anything to hurt Scarlet, I'll kill you myself… slowly." She smiles sweetly while rubbing her round belly, as if she didn't just threaten me with a violent death. I guess she is a Rossi after all.

"I swear I won't do anything to hurt her," I promise. Quite the opposite; I would do anything to keep her safe.

Aspen nods, seemingly satisfied by my response, she takes Quinton's hand and pulls him away. I watch them walk out of the dining room before following them a moment later.

I walk upstairs to the guest room that has become mine. I'm only a few doors away from Scarlet's room and the dirty fantasy she put in my mind runs rampant in my head. I wonder if she is taking a shower right now, touching her wet little pussy thinking about me. Is she moaning my name? I'm so curious, I almost walk past my door to get to hers.

Forcing myself to behave, I stop at my room and open the door. I walk in thinking about taking a quick shower myself. It's probably a good idea with my cock being so hard. Cold shower it is, I decide.

Peeling my clothes off quickly, I make my way into the attached bathroom, turning on the cold water in the shower. I step under the spray right away, letting the icy water cool my heated skin. I stand under the spray until my dick is completely deflated, and my muscles ache from the cold.

When I step out, I wrap myself up in one of the large, fluffy white towels. This is much nicer than downstairs. I'm glad Xander trusts me enough by now to let me spend my time up here. And with no stress to worry about, I hope River won't appear again anytime soon.

Thinking of my split personality makes me remember the notebook the doctor gave me. With everything going on, I haven't had a chance to even look at it. I haven't written anything in there myself, but I wonder if River has.

I dry off my hair and pull on a pair of sweats before I seek out the notebook sitting on my bedside table. I open it up and see my familiar handwriting on the first page.

R*en*,

I'm starting to think she likes me more than you. Why else would she come so hard when I fingered her through the bars? She was so fucking wet for me when I called her my little slut and promised next time I would fuck her ass. Maybe you need to fuck her better and then she'll tell you all her secrets like she tells me. Unless she's told you about the baby growing inside her already.

River

I read the note twice, then a third time, letting the words sink in slowly. There is too much to digest in these few lines, and they're so monumental I'm not sure if I can believe them.

Did my angel really lie to me again? Betrayal settles in my

stomach like a deadly poison. Jealousy, shock, and a sense of loss mingles in my chest. I don't know what to think or what to believe. Can Scarlet really be pregnant with my child? We didn't use protection, and we had plenty of sex, but why wouldn't she tell me, and why would she tell him? Does she really like that side of me better? The bad side? Does she like it when I hurt her and degrade her? Or is River simply playing mind games again? Although he hasn't lied to me, at least not that I know of. Could this really be true?

My mind spins. And it won't stop until I know the truth.

23
SCARLET

Freshly showered, I dress in the cutest pajamas I can find. They are not as sexy as I hoped, but it's not like I have lingerie lying around here. Plus, I still have to walk out in the hallway, and sneaking to Ren's room is risky enough without being half naked.

My hair is still damp when I put it up in a ponytail and exit my room quietly. On tiptoes, I walk down the dark hall to Ren's room. I look left and right quickly, making sure no one is out here before I grab the door handle. The brass is cold against my warm hand as I turn the knob slowly until I hear the lock disengage.

I step into the dimly lit room, excitement filling my veins when I see a shirtless Ren sitting on the bed waiting for me. I close the door as softly as I can, locking it behind me just in case. Only when I spin back around to look at Ren, do I notice the dark expression on his face. His eyes are hooded, with an eerie shadow under them. His lips are pulled into a thin line, and his jaw is set tightly, as if he is grinding his teeth.

"River," I whisper hesitantly, wondering if locking the door was a mistake.

"No, it's me, but I guess you'd prefer it the other way," Ren says darkly, while confusing the hell out of me.

"What's that supposed to mean? Of course I want it to be you." I take a few steps toward the bed, eating up the distance between us with each step.

"Are you sure about that?"

"Ren, what is this about? Please talk to me."

"Why didn't you tell me River fingered you? Is it because you enjoyed it too much?"

My face heats up with embarrassment. The short answer is yes, he is right. I didn't tell him because I'm ashamed how much I enjoyed it.

"Cat got your tongue?" Ren taunts.

"Yes, River fingered me through the bars when he grabbed me. Yes, I enjoyed it more than I am willing to admit to anyone… maybe even to myself. I'm sorry, I should have told you."

"Is there more you should have told me?" Ren questions through gritted teeth. I notice his hands are balled into tight fists next to him. A vein pulsing on his forehead. Why is he so angry?

"No, nothing else happened," I say, my voice trembling slightly. My answer seems to only enrage him more. He gets up from the bed with a grunt, his muscles stiff as he paces through the room, only a few feet away from me. The tension in the room is high. If I had a knife, I could cut it, or maybe I need a knife to protect myself instead.

I'm so confused by his actions, all I can do is stand there like a deer caught in headlights.

"Don't fucking lie to me, Scarlet. Tell me your secret."

"I don't have a secret," I defend. "I don't understand why you get so mad if River touches me. It's still you, Ren. You are River, it's your eyes I'm looking into, your hands on my skin. You act like I'm cheating on you, but I'm not. I love you, every part of you."

"Stop lying and tell me the truth." Ren yells at me so loudly I take a step backward.

"I don't… I don't understand…" I really don't know what to say. What does he want me to tell him? "I don't know what you want from me, but I'm not staying here so you can yell at me. I'm going back to my room until you calm down."

I spin around and head for the door. A shiver runs down my spine when I hear Ren's footsteps approaching. I reach for the doorknob, but before the cool brass meets my skin, Ren grabs me by the back of the neck and pulls me toward him. A scream threatens to rip from my throat as a hand slaps over my mouth.

A sinister laugh comes from behind me. "Fuck, that was just too easy." I know right away I'm dealing with River now. It's the sinister edge in his voice, the cruel way his fingers dig into my neck, and the way I'm yanked back against his chest. "Ren is so fucking predictable, just a little push of a button, and he loses control. And you, *Angel*. What am I going to do with you today?"

Fear slithers through my body like a dangerous snake. How far would River go to hurt me? The question evaporates into thin air when he pulls me closer to his body, grinding his erection into my ass. Maybe he doesn't want to hurt me after all. I think it's something else he has on his mind.

"Mhh, no bars between us today. So many things I want to do to you," he whispers into my ear, his minty breath fanning over my cheek.

Another shiver runs through my body, but this time not because of fear. He lifts the hand from my mouth, only to run his palm down my body. "Let's face it, you won't scream, no matter what I do to you. You wouldn't want your precious Ren to get in trouble."

He grabs my breast roughly, pinching my nipple through my shirt, making me gasp in surprise.

"You like this, my little whore? You like me touching you however I please? Tell me how wet your cunt is right now, how your clit is begging to be touched."

"Why? Why do you care if I like this or not?" I don't know why I feel like taunting him, but some depraved part of myself wants to see how far I can push him.

"I don't really care," he growls, "I'd fuck you even if you begged me to stop. But I like you admitting what a dirty little slut you are. And I like even more knowing that Ren hates it when I touch you." There must be something very wrong with me because his twisted words only turn me on more. I feel my pussy growing wet, my core tightens, and my thighs quiver in anticipation.

His hand moves from my breast to my stomach, stopping right over my belly button.

"Please," I beg breathlessly, letting my head fall back to rest on River's shoulder.

"Please what? Please stop or please fuck me?" River taunts.

"Please fuck me," I shamelessly admit. "I want you."

"Prove it." He suddenly lets go of me. His hands disappear from my body, and he steps away, leaving me unsteady on my own feet. When I turn around a bit disoriented, I find him climbing onto the bed, laying down with his head propped up on the pillow. "Come and ride my cock. Show me how much you want me," he challenges.

Without thinking, I grab the hem of my pj shirt and pull it over my head. I dig my fingers into the waistband of my bottoms and pull those down together with my underwear. River's eyes are filled with lust as he undoes his pants and pulls his already hard cock out.

I don't waste any time climbing onto the bed with him. I straddle his lap, positioning my pussy over him until his head is nudging against my entrance. I lower myself slowly, apparently too slow for River.

He grabs hold of my hips and slams me down on his cock, impaling me with a sharp pain. I hiss at the discomfort while River groans in pleasure. "Fuck, you feel so good. You were made for me." His words somehow ease the pain a bit.

He lets me adjust to his size for a few moments, but his hungry eyes never leave mine. When the discomfort has eased, I start moving my hips a little, testing at first, then a little more. River groans again, while his thumb finds my clit to rub small circles over it. I can feel myself growing wet, making him slide in and out of me smoothly as I bounce my hips up and down.

    Closing my eyes, I let my head fall back to enjoy the euphoric sensation of us fucking, and River keeping pressure on my small bundle of nerves between my legs. He rubs it relentlessly while meeting my hips with every stroke until I'm nothing more than a moaning mess about to have a mindblowing orgasm.

    "I want you to come all over my cock, I want to feel you squeeze me while you fall apart." He pulls his hand back an inch and slaps my clit with his palm. I squeal out in surprise, shocked by the new sensation. Before I can comprehend what he is doing, he slaps my pussy again, and the sharp sting is what sends me over the edge.

    "That's it, my little slut. Come for me, squeeze my cock with your pretty little cunt." My orgasm slams into me suddenly and violently, while River continues the onslaught on my clit. Pleasure like never before courses through my veins, and my whole body stiffens with the release before every muscle inside of me turns into jelly.

    I crumble down like a paper doll, too exhausted to hold myself up. My cheek is pressed against River's chest. My mouth hangs open, and I breathe heavily to catch my breath. I might be slobbering, but I couldn't care less. My mind is too consumed with the unbelievable pleasure I just experienced. I'm still not fully conscious yet when River shifts beneath me, flipping us over so that I'm on the bottom, facing him.

Opening my eyes, I catch the darkness in River's gaze. A darkness that makes me shiver with both fear and anticipation. How does he make me feel this way? I should be frightened, but instead, his darkness sets my core ablaze in a way Ren can't. The thought alone confuses me beyond measures. I need to stop thinking about them as two separate people. River is Ren, Ren is River. Two sides of the same coin.

Before I can think too much into it, River grins mischievously, and his eyes gleam with excitement. I'm about to ask him what he is thinking about when he grabs my hips and flips me around on my stomach.

He straddles the back of my legs. I can feel his heavy cock laying on my wet thighs. "I'm going to go slow, but it might still hurt a bit. I'll try to stretch you out first."

Oh, my god. He is going to fuck my ass, I realize. Part of me wants to object, but the other deprived part wants to let him do it.

"Reach back and spread your ass cheeks for me." My mind is still processing what he is asking when a sharp slap on my ass makes me move faster. Reaching back, I spread my cheeks for him. "Good whore," he praises. His palm finds my now tender skin again, but this time, he simply rubs the spot, massaging it until I forget the pain completely.

I'm so exposed to him, showing him the most private part of myself as he continues to massage my butt cheeks. My whole body is hyper aware, all my nerve endings buzzing with excitement as his thumb finds my asshole. At first, he just massages it but when I feel him spit on my hole, I know more is to come soon.

He presses the tip of his thumb inside of me. The sensation is foreign, but it doesn't hurt like I expected. He probes my hole with his thumb going in and out slowly before suddenly slipping out completely. He doesn't leave me empty for long, replacing his thumb with two of his fingers. Once he's worked those fingers inside of me, he spreads them apart, stretching me in the process.

"How does it feel to have my fingers in your ass, preparing you for my cock?"

"Good," I moan without thinking, making River chuckle behind me.

"Are you ready for my cock?"

"I don't know." His fingers are much smaller than his dick.

"I'll guess we're about to find out," River taunts, removing his fingers from my hole. He spits on it one more time before I feel the smooth head of his cock at my back entrance. "Try to stay relaxed."

He pushes inside slowly, but the pressure builds quickly. I was right; his cock is much bigger than his fingers, and my hole feels like it's about to rip open. I whimper, digging my nails into my skin to absorb some of the pain.

The head of his cock slips inside, and I will my muscles to relax. He goes very slowly, but somehow, it's not slow enough.

It isn't until he starts talking again that I forget about the discomfort. "My good little slut is taking it up the ass so well.

Just like I knew you would. All whores like getting fucked in the ass. How does it feel, *Angel?*"

"Full... so full..." I manage to get out.

"Good, I like you full of my cock. I like your holes good and stuffed. I'm gonna start fucking you, and you're going to be a good little girl and keep those ass cheeks spread for me." His voice is husky, like he is barely hanging on to his restraint.

I nod into the pillow, holding myself open for him as he starts to move in and out of my ass at a steady pace. It doesn't take long for the pain to completely subside and a new kind of pleasure to set it.

"Fuck yes, that's it, slut, relax for me. Let me fuck you." At his words, I relax a little further, sinking into the mattress.

He increases his pace, fucking me faster and harder with each stroke. The longer he goes, the better it feels, and before I know it, I press my ass up, urging him to go even deeper.

"I'm going to fill your ass with my come, but I want you to come with me. I want you to fall apart while I fuck your ass." River snakes his arms around me until his fingers are right over my clit. He rubs the small bundle of nerves roughly, and it only takes a few seconds for my orgasm to sneak up on me.

"I—I'm coming..." I manage to spit out between moans.

River grunts behind me, fucking me in deep strokes while pinching my clit so hard I see stars. My thighs quiver, and my body tightens as my release takes hold of me.

"Fuck yes, milk my cock!" River roars as I come all over

his fingers. Pleasure runs through every vein in my body, making me forget I'm with River and how wrong this is.

He stiffens with a groan, and I can feel his cock pulsating inside of me. His orgasm wrecks his body just as mine slowly fades out.

River collapses on top of me, pressing me into the mattress. We're both breathing heavily, trying to catch our breath. He rolls off me, lying on his back next to me.

For a few minutes, neither one of us says anything.

"Was that prove enough?" I ask, breaking the silence.

"I have to admit, you did pretty good."

"Now you have no reason left to be angry. I've proven that I love you, and Rebecca is finally dead."

"What?" He asks, like he doesn't know what I'm talking about. It dawns on me that he doesn't know about the whole New Haven Operation.

"Rebecca and her son are dead," I tell him along with the rest of the story. He listens intently, only asking a few questions here and there.

When I'm done filling him in on everything, he sits up in his bed. "It was supposed to be me," he says angrily. "I was supposed to kill her."

"What does it matter who did it? She is dead, and that's all that matters." I try to reason with him, but he is getting more agitated by the second. I get up from the bed and start getting dressed, feeling vulnerable in my naked form.

"You just don't understand. It should have been me. It was *my* revenge!"

"You scare me when you get angry like this," I admit, hoping that my statement will calm him down. It doesn't.

"Good, you should be scared."

"Maybe I should tell my dad to put you back in the cell," I warn, but we both know I'm just bluffing.

"Maybe you should go back to your room and keep your pretty little mouth shut."

"Maybe I should. It appears you enjoy being alone."

"Finally, you get it."

Leaving him like this might be a terrible idea. But what else am I supposed to do? He clearly doesn't want me here anymore. I don't know what I expected him to do? Cuddle?

"Fine, I'll leave you alone for now, but don't try anything stupid. There are guards everywhere, and they know you are not supposed to leave."

"Yeah, yeah, I get it. I'm still a prisoner." River is still sitting on the bed, only a thin sheet covering him up. I walk over to stand next to him. He looks up at me in confusion. "What do you think you're doing?"

I dip my head down and place a chaste kiss on his cheek. "Kissing you goodnight."

He looks at me in surprise but doesn't say anything as I straighten back up and make my way across the room. "I love you," I tell him without turning around, before opening the door and slipping out of the room. He might not care about hearing it, but I'll say it no matter what.

24
SCARLET

The bright, glaring sunshine streaming through my bedroom window is like a sad joke. Mother Nature is making fun of me. Rubbing it in by reminding me how beautiful the world can be, when inside, I feel nothing but darkness as I go through the motions of brushing my teeth and getting dressed.

It's always the same question rolling through my head like a wave. Who will I see today? Ren or River?

It's almost too much for me to wrap my head around the morning after being with River. Does Ren know? Is it cheating to sleep with somebody when they're the other half of the same person you've loved for as long as you can remember? Because I hardly remember a time when Ren wasn't important to me, and River was inside him all along. Even if neither of us knew it. But does that make me innocent, or is it only a convenient loophole? It's not like I initiated things. I only wish I knew what would calm Ren down if he's hurt.

He had an appointment scheduled with Dr. Stone today, and by the time I approach Ren's room, she's coming out. There's nothing in her expression to give me a clue how things went—not that she would go into specifics. I wouldn't ask her to, either, no matter how much I wish she would. I can't invade the privacy of their sessions.

That leaves me with nothing to do but offer her a tight smile that doesn't last very long. "Who did you see today?" I ask, glancing toward the closed door. "Is he Ren or River?" And did he tell you what he did to me yesterday?

The doctor's kind eyes soften before she pats my arm. "Ren. I spoke to Ren. He seems all right today."

I can practically taste my relief as my body loosens a little now that some of the tension can drain away. "Okay. That's good to know." I can breathe easier as I continue down the hall and knock gently at the closed door. I still have to be careful. It's one thing for Ren to behave himself while he's talking to the doctor, but she's not the one who betrayed him yesterday—if he sees it as a betrayal.

He only grunts in response to my knock. He has to know it's me. Once again, a sense of dread washes over me, and I open the door with my heart in my throat. How much more of this roller coaster can I take?

He's sitting on the foot of the bed, and nearby is a small armchair. The doctor must have pulled it closer to him before they started their session. I move slowly toward it, trying to read him as I cross the room. "How did the session go?" I wish I didn't sound so nervous, but I can't help it. I don't know what to expect. He could be Ren right now, but River tends to take control at the drop of a hat.

"What, the doctor didn't tell you all about it?" The resentment hanging heavy in his voice is a hand wrapping itself around my heart and squeezing tight. He knows. I feel it. And right away, I am almost overcome by the impulse to apologize and beg his forgiveness.

"You know there's only so much she can tell me. I'm not trying to pry." Maybe it's not such a great idea to sit close to him, but I'm not going to run away in fear. I love him too much for that.

Once I'm perched carefully in the chair, he lifts his head and hits me with a flat stare. There is so much swirling in his dark eyes. "So, was it fun? Did you enjoy yourself?"

I will not cry. I won't shrink away, either. "What do you mean?"

"He left me a note. River. He told me what you two did." All at once, he almost jumps to his feet, and I lean back in the chair when instinct tells me to stay out of his way. I will not run. I am not going to run away from him, now or ever. Still, he's not making it easy to stay put while he walks around clenching and unclenching his fists.

"I can explain," I offer in a whisper.

"Oh, you can explain. Like that's going to change anything." His snide laughter is so much like River's, it makes me shudder.

"It won't change anything, but it might help you understand. I bet he made it sound like I went running to him or something because we had a fight. Right? He probably tried to rub it in your face." I've already been through all of this in my head, practicing it in bed while I knew he was busy in his session. It's like a script by now, something I've memorized and can rattle off, even while he stares at me with so much pain etched across his handsome face. Practice was the only way I knew I could get through this.

Though even now, it's not easy to keep my head held high under the weight of his accusatory stare. "That's not how it was at all. He turned into River during our fight."

He turns his back on me, staring out the window. "Is that when you told him about the baby?"

All the air in my lungs rushes out of me at once. That bastard. "He told you about that?" I whisper while my heart breaks.

"Do you think maybe I deserved to hear about it?"

"I only told him…" A tear slips down my cheek, and I rub it away, my voice breaking, before I manage to catch my breath and try again. "I told him because I guess I was hoping I could protect myself that way. I wasn't trying to keep it from you, seriously. You have to believe me."

"What about now?" I catch his profile, silhouetted against the glaring sunlight when he turns his head to the side. "Would you have told me about the baby if he hadn't forced your hand? What are we going to do?"

"We don't have to worry about it. I was wrong." Not now. Please, not now. I don't want to break down. I don't want to make this more complicated. And for all I know, the sight of me weeping could bring River to the surface. He seems to enjoy it when I'm in pain.

"So you're not pregnant?" I wish I could tell whether he's glad or not.

My head swings back and forth before I manage to speak. "I assumed I was, that's all. But I took a test, and it was negative. So there goes that."

A few heavy, silent moments pass before he asks, "How do you feel about it?"

"I'll get over it." I'm trying. I really am. But grief doesn't follow our schedules.

"You… wanted the baby?"

I hate the disbelief I hear coming from him. How can he doubt me? "I mean, I was a little freaked out when I first thought I might be pregnant," I admit. "But… I don't know. It would have grown a piece of us inside of me. I guess I didn't know how much I wanted to do that until I saw the negative test. I know it doesn't make any sense."

He's quiet for a long time before he finally grunts. "No. It does. But now, you're not tied down to me, so that's a plus." There's a bitter note running through his words.

"Don't say that."

"It's the truth. What the fuck would you want to be tied down to me for? Besides," he adds, turning away again, "it might be a little awkward, fucking River while you're, like, eight or nine months pregnant. Right? It's more convenient this way."

"That's just not true."

Whirling on me, he growls, "The second River shows up, you fuck him. I mean, what is there to not understand? Do you think I'm stupid?"

"No! But you're letting him twist you up. That's what he wants. Dammit!"

I close my eyes and count to five, taking a slow, measured breath with every count. This is Ren, and I love Ren, and it would shatter my heart if I said anything I couldn't take back.

Once I trust myself again, I murmur, "He wants you to be jealous. Don't give him what he wants."

"How am I not supposed to be jealous? You fucked him!"

"I had sex with you," I insist. "I don't consider it that way. Like you're separate people. Because you aren't, not really. You're the same person, and I love you."

He barks out a nasty laugh that makes me want to die. There's so much hatred and ugliness in it. "I'm really glad you can tell yourself that."

There's no stopping the tears, no matter how I try. Let him see how he's hurting me. How I mean what I'm saying. "I can't believe you would accuse me like this! Like I'm trying to justify cheating on you or something."

"That's exactly what you're doing!"

"River is part of you," I snap. "I love you just the same, no matter what mental state you happen to be in. Whether it's you or River in there. I love you. I was with you yesterday."

He drops back to the bed and lowers his head until it's resting in his hands. "It's not the same. I'm not… there when it happens. He might be part of me, but he's not me." There is so much hurt in the way he says it. He's in pain, and I'm part of the reason why he is in pain, and there's nothing I can do about it. It's the most helpless feeling in the world. It makes me sick to my stomach, but no matter how miserable I am, it's nothing compared to what he feels.

"I'm sorry," I whisper, even when I know it doesn't make a difference. You can't put the toothpaste back in the tube.

"Yeah. Me, too." With a grunt, he shakes his head and lets his hands drop to his lap. "There's only one thing to do about this."

I don't like the sound of it, but I nod anyway. He deserves to have his say.

"I need you to stay away from me." When my mouth falls open, he holds up a hand and looks at the floor. "I need some time to myself. That's all. And if you truly give a shit about me, you'll let me have it. No fighting."

I do truly love him. In a world full of doubts and fears, that's one thing I never have to question. It's the reason I'm able to stand on trembling legs. "Okay. I'll give you your space."

I want to tell him again how sorry I am, but he doesn't need to hear it now. If anything, the sound of my voice is hurting him. It seems like all I can do lately is hurt him. "I guess… send word when you think you can handle seeing me again. I won't bother you," I promise, even as my instincts scream at me to stay and make him listen. I can't bully him into believing me. I can only trust he'll see the truth on his own.

I might not have been able to keep myself from crying,

but I'm at least able to hold back the first sob until I'm out of the room, leaning against the wall for support with both hands clamped over my mouth to muffle the sound.

25
REN

I don't love the silence in the room after I've finished telling Dr. Stone about what went down with Scarlet. It's the kind of silence that weighs on a guy. I know she's got to be thinking all sorts of shit she doesn't want to say out loud. And I fucking hate it. Somehow, in the middle of all this shit, it's what I hate the most.

"Well?" I have to ask. "What do you think? You're not saying anything, and that's not a good sign."

"Forgive me." There are times I hate how gentle and careful she always is. She doesn't want to say the wrong thing. Always wanting to be professional. I get it, and when I'm not in a shit mood, I can even appreciate it. It can't be easy, sitting there and acting like a blank slate for a patient to scrawl their thoughts and fears across. There's got to be all kinds of opinions banging around inside her skull, but she's good at pretending otherwise.

Sitting up a little straighter, she clears her throat. "What you're telling me is, Scarlet became physically involved with River while he was at the forefront of your consciousness."

"Pretty much, yeah. She knew it was River and not me, but she did it anyway. And she didn't even apologize." Or did she? Fuck, it's all screwed up in my head. I wasn't thinking clearly. It's not so easy to piece everything together in the right order when I was practically blind with rage and hurt.

"Do you believe Scarlet deliberately waited for River to come out before she initiated the physical interaction with him?"

The question makes me way too uncomfortable. Like my skin is too tight for my body all of a sudden and somebody bumped up the thermostat. "I don't know," I admit.

"I'm not asking what you think is true," she continues in that soft, even voice. "I'm asking what first went through your mind when you found out the two of them were intimate. Did you imagine her preferring River to you?"

I might not have thought of it that way at the time, but now that she mentions it… "Yeah. I think that's where my brain went right away."

"Has she refused physical contact with you?"

"No," I admit. I wish she wouldn't look at me the way she is now, like she's trying to see inside my head. "It's not like that."

"Has she expressed more of an interest in the River side of your personality than in you, yourself?"

"No," I mutter. My head is starting to hurt from all of this. "I don't know what I'm thinking."

"You're thinking she cheated on you."

"Well, yeah." Hearing the words spoken out loud is ugly, but I can't pretend the feelings aren't there.

I throw my hands into the air, staring at her. "Well? What do you think? Because she was hurt by the way I reacted, and I can't look at her right now. It can't go on like this forever."

She blows out a long breath, frowning, and I get the feeling I'm not going to like what I'm about to hear. "Ren, at the end of the day, you need to keep in mind what we've discussed many times during our sessions. I realize it doesn't feel like River is part of you, but that is the way you need to begin thinking of him. You are not two separate entities."

"So you're saying she's right?"

"It isn't as simple as that." I almost hate how gentle she is. The understanding doctor. "Whether you are acting as Ren or as River, Scarlet sees the same person. And if you are ever going to heal after everything you've been through, you must find a way to begin seeing him as yourself."

"You make it sound so easy."

"I know it's not easy," she insists. "But it is part of the process. The most important part. If you are going to move forward in your life, this is a crucial step. Shifting your mindset."

She checks her watch. I recognize her regretful frown. "And that's it for today. I urge you to give this more thought. Don't be afraid to think of River as part of yourself. Can you give this some real thought before we meet again?"

"Sure. What else do I have to do?" After all, I'm still a prisoner. Just because I'm not downstairs in a cell doesn't mean I'm free to go wherever I want. It's okay for me to wander around the house, but I don't feel comfortable doing it. There are always eyes on me, like the family's guards. Some of them were with us when we went to rescue Luna. They know I'm not going to hurt anybody around here, and they saw me throw myself over Q to keep him from being killed. That's still not enough to erase the distrust I see in all of them as I walk through the house after my session, looking for Xander.

Like I told Dr. Stone, there's nothing for me to do but think, and I've had more on my mind than just Scarlet and River since we came back from rescuing Luna. Rebecca might be dead, but that's not the end of it. I was stupid to ever think it would be. Somehow, I should've known she had backing from dangerous people.

It's no big surprise, finding Xander in his office. The briefest frown touches his face before he catches himself and clears his throat. "What can I do for you? Dr. Stone walked past a few minutes ago. Did your session go well?"

"It was fine." He might be paying for my treatment, but that doesn't mean I have to share with him. Not the specifics, anyway. "That's not what I came in to talk to you about."

"I'm all ears." Yeah, and he's all nerves, too. I make him nervous. Part of me wants to shout boo and freak him out a little, since I don't think there are many people who have ever seen him look as uncomfortable as he does right now.

I point to one of the chairs in front of his desk, and he nods before I take a seat. Leaning forward with my elbows on my knees, I ask, "What's next? How do we take down those Russians running operations out of New Haven?"

His eyebrows shoot up, but that's the only reaction that shows on his face. "What makes you so sure we're going to take them down?"

He can be a real prick when he puts his mind to it. "What's the alternative? Leaving all those people there? They didn't do anything to deserve being under the thumb of those assholes. We can't leave them high and dry."

He takes his time drawing a breath, while all I can do is bite my tongue to keep from screaming at him to start talking. "I see what you're saying," he begins. In a way, he reminds me of Dr. Stone right now. Like he's walking through a minefield and wants to be careful where he steps. I hate it, but I guess I understand.

"But?" I prompt when he leaves me hanging for too long.

"But it's not that simple. We go in there, guns blazing, and we start a war. You have to know that?"

Bitter disappointment burns its way through my esophagus, leaving a bad taste in my mouth. It's so easy for him to sit back and say things like that. "Those people need us."

"Ren, I need you to remember something. I know you want to put an end to all of this, and nobody has more of a reason than you. You have lost so much, and I am truly sorry. But let's not fool ourselves, either."

"What does that mean?"

He barely stops short of rolling his eyes. "It means we are not the good guys here. We aren't heroes. There's no charging in and saving the world. I need you to remember that."

"So, what?" I can't be bothered to hide my disappointment, dropping back into the chair. "We stay here and do nothing? How can we?"

"And how can I start a war with the Russians?" he counters. "That sort of thing is expensive, and not only in terms of dollars and cents. It means losing people. And that will happen, no matter how prepared we are."

I can't believe it. It's like being in a nightmare. Screaming as loud as I can, but unable to make a sound. With no one to take me seriously, with no way of changing anything. I have no choice but to sit on my hands and be a good boy, while Xander calls the shots. And so many people could be suffering this very minute, maybe even worse than I ever did.

"There is something I wanted to discuss with you." He folds his hands on top of the desk, hitting me with a heavy stare. "I understand Scarlet has been very upset ever since the two of you had a fight. I don't like to get involved in her personal life if I can help it, but I need to know I can trust the two of you alone together."

"I'm never going to hurt her," I promise, though the words feel flat and empty in my mouth. Because I can't really make that promise, can I? Considering I'm not always in control of myself.

"It seems as though you already have, but I understand what you mean," he replies with a sigh. "Don't make me regret giving you a little more freedom. That's all I'm trying to say."

"I get it. I'm trying to give her some space to figure things out for herself. I'm trying to do the same thing. That's the most I can tell you," I conclude with a shrug.

"That's generally the best way to go about it," he agrees, nodding slowly. "It's never good to fly off half-cocked in the heat of the moment. You always end up saying things you wish you hadn't."

I'm afraid we're already past that point, but I won't bother admitting it. Besides, footsteps interrupt us before I get the chance, and I turn in the chair in time to see Q strolling into the room. Something has changed between us ever since I took that bullet for him. He won't come out and say it, and I don't expect him to, but there's been a definite shift in the way he acts around me. There are no more dirty looks, or comments, no tension.

"Sorry. What did I interrupt?" He freezes halfway into the room, eyes darting back and forth between me and his dad.

"I think we were in the process of wrapping up our discussion." Xander lifts an eyebrow, and I nod in agreement.

"Good. I was looking for you, actually," Q tells me, coming to a stop in front of the desk and leaning his ass against it, arms folded. "Do you wanna go out? Grab a couple of beers?"

I must be missing something. "You mean it?" I look at Xander, but his face is blank. I can't tell what he thinks about the idea.

Q glances over his shoulder like he's checking in with Xander. "I mean, you should get out sometime. You must be going nuts, being stuck here."

Interesting choice of words. "I don't know," I mumble, which is the truth. I don't know if it's a good idea for me to be out in public where anything could happen. This is what my life has become. Afraid to leave the house in case the other side of my personality decides to come out and wreak havoc.

It's pretty clear he is not taking no for an answer. I know him better than to think he will now that he's made up his mind. And it wouldn't be bad to get out for a little while, either—I'm sick of looking at the same walls.

"Okay," I agree, though my heart is nowhere near in it. "If it's all right, yeah, I'll come out with you."

"You don't need to sound like you accepted a death sentence." He snickers.

That's just it. Lately, it feels like my whole life is a death sentence. I guess I need a night out more than I thought I did.

26
SCARLET

"What do you mean they went out?"

"Out, as in they went to a bar to drink some beers," Aspen explains, like it's not a big deal at all.

"But why? I mean, other than to find girls. Do you think Ren is done with me?" I'm almost certain that I'm overreacting… almost.

"I think you worry too much." Aspen laughs. "They are just letting off some steam. Ren has been stressed, and Quinton is dealing with a lot too. He thought he lost his best friend forever and now he is back. Let them spend some time together and trust that they don't do anything stupid."

"I trust them; it's everyone else I don't trust. What if some skanks just walk up to them and stick their tongues down their throats? What if someone roofies them and steals their kidneys?"

"I think you watch too much TV." Aspen waves me off like I'm crazy.

"Maybe you don't watch enough true crime!" I snap back. Does she not know about all the crazy people out there?

"The guys can take care of themselves, Scarlet. You don't have to worry."

"And what if Ren turns to River while they are out? River might still want to hurt Q." That finally gets her attention. "I'm the only one who knows how to deal with River!"

"River hasn't made an appearance in a few days. I think Ren has it under control now."

"I had a run-in with River two days ago, and the reason Ren is more in control here is because there is nothing to aggravate him. What if some drunk picks a fight with him? That's all it would take."

"All right, now you've got me worried too," Aspen admits, biting her bottom lip.

"Do you know what bar they went to?" I ask.

"Yes, but I'll only tell you if you promise not to go alone?"

"I'll take a driver and a guard with me." Now that he re-implanted the tracker under my skin, my dad gives me pretty much free rein on when and where I can go.

"All right," she says, but her eyes are still guarded, like she's not sure that this is a good idea. "They went to TopShot; it's a small bar, downtown Main Street."

"Thank you!" I give Aspen a quick hug and kiss on the cheek before I leave her room and make my way down the hall.

"Be careful!" She yells after me, a hint of worry in her soft voice.

"I will," I yell back over my shoulder as I hurry into my

room to grab my purse and slip into some high heel boots that go great with my skinny jeans and leather jacket. When I'm all dressed, I leave my room and make my way downstairs.

Once I'm in the foyer, I stand in front of Tony, one of the younger guards, who looks at me curiously. "I need you to come with me and be my bodyguard at a bar."

"All right." He bobs his head. "When are we leaving?"

"Now."

Tony nods again and follows me out the front door, where one of my dad's drivers is usually standing by. I get into the back seat while Tony takes the front. I tell the driver where to go, and he takes off right away.

Thirty minutes later, we arrive in front of the bar. The driver parks, and Tony gets out to open my door for me. I step out into the cool city air.

"Thank you," I tell him while staring at two girls in short dresses and high heels that enter the bar.

I look down at my plain jeans and boots, wondering if I should have dressed up a little more to fit in here.

"Don't worry, they are just skanks. You look nice," Tony says before clearing his throat nervously. "Sorry, I shouldn't have said that. I didn't mean it like it sounded."

"You're fine, thanks." I've known Tony for a while, and he has never been anything but courteous to me.

"So what's the plan?" Tony questions.

"Can you wait outside the door while I go in there and spy on… ahm… I mean." Shit, I can't think of a good excuse.

"While you spy on your brother and your boyfriend?"

Tony finishes my sentence.

"Oh well. Yes." I shrug. I guess the cat is out of the bag already.

"I'll only let you in there on your own because I know they are here too, but I still want you to text or call me if you need me to come in. Let me have your phone, and I'll type in my number." He holds his hand out to me, and I dig my phone out of my purse to hand to him. He quickly saves his number and hands me my cell back.

I thank him again before making my way inside the bar. I step into the dingy space, the smell of alcohol and sweat hits me right away. It's pretty packed in here, which is not surprising on a Friday night. Scanning the space, I find Quinton and Ren sitting at the bar with their backs turned toward me. I sigh in release when I see no girls next to them.

Looking around, I find an empty table in the corner of the room, and I walk over to take a seat there. I slide into the booth, realizing the table is sticky from spilled drinks. I briefly think about sitting somewhere else, but I don't think another table would be any different. Plus, from here I can watch the guys perfectly through the crowd. I feel like some secret agent on a mission. Keeping my head down, I make sure they won't see me even if they happen to look my way.

About 15 minutes pass, and I realize being a secret agent on a stakeout is not much fun. Matter-of-fact, it is pretty boring because Ren and Q have barely moved. They simply sit at the bar talking to each other and drinking beers.

I don't know what I was so worried about. It was a stupid idea to come, I finally realize. I'm about to get up from my seat and leave this place when I catch sight of a woman in a mini-dress, making a beeline toward Ren and Q.

My whole body stiffens as I watch my nightmare come true. The beautiful black-haired woman takes a seat next to Ren—my Ren. She lifts her hand and touches his forearm to get his attention. Ren immediately pulls his arm away from her touch, but she doesn't seem to get the message. I don't know what she is saying, but it looks like she is giggling and touching his upper arm now. Red hot jealousy courses through my veins at the near sight of some woman touching what's mine.

Someone moves into my view, making me get up so hastily that I bump my knees against the table. Cursing the pain away, I slide out of the booth, ready to confront the woman who is trying to seduce my boyfriend, when some guy steps into my way.

"Where are you going so fast, beautiful?" the young man slurs. He looks like one of the college frat guys at MIT.

"None of your business," I snap back impatiently. I don't have time for this. I try to push past him, but he shifts so he is in my way again, forcing me to bump into him.

"That was rude. I was just asking you a question. No reason to be such a bitch." He takes a step toward me, and I have nowhere else to go than to step back.

Panic bubbles inside of me as I try to look past him. He takes another threatening step toward me, his hand coming up to touch my face. I slap his arm away, which only makes him angry. He snatches my wrist and starts pulling me toward the bathrooms.

"Stop!" I yell, but the loud music and chatter drowns my voice out. I really regret coming here. I'm just about to freak out when I see a large form coming from the side.

Before I know it, the guy dragging me releases my wrist. "Hey, man, we were just having a little fun—" That's all he gets out before Tony's fist connects with his face. The guy's eyes roll back, and he falls to his knees.

"Are you okay?" Tony asks, patting my arm lightly.

"Um, yeah. I'm fine…"

"What the fuck are you doing here?" My brother's voice meets my ear, making me flinch. I'm in so much trouble.

Hesitantly, I turn around to face him. Quinton and Ren have made their way across the bar and are standing only a foot away from me now. Both have their arms crossed over their chest, scolding me as if I'm a misbehaving kid.

I straighten my spine and roll my shoulders back. "I was just out having a drink. I'm an adult, and I brought a bodyguard," I say, as if that is a perfect excuse to be here.

"And you just happen to be at the same bar we are?" Ren lifts his eyebrows.

"I know. What a coincidence." I try to laugh it off, but neither Ren nor Quinton join in with my laughter. Even Tony has turned stoic. "Okay, fine. I came to check on you, but only because I was worried."

A grunt from the floor safes me from the guys' deathly stare. Quinton looks down at the guy at the ground. "Looks like you are the only one we have to worry about. What happened here?"

"He is drunk and got a little handsy. Tony took care of it."

"Thank you, Tony. Sorry my sister drug you out here. Can you take care of this guy while we take her home?"

"My pleasure," Tony replies before giving the guy on the floor his attention. "Get up, asshole, or I'll drag you out back."

"Let's go," Ren orders so roughly, that for a moment, I wonder if he is actually River. He grabs my hand and starts tugging me toward the door. I don't object. I simply follow, content with the fact that he is holding my hand.

Quinton is right behind us as we make our way outside. Just before we exit the bar, I catch sight of the woman hitting on Ren earlier. Her curious eyes following us. Feeling a bit reckless, I lift my hand and give her the middle finger. Her mouth pops open in shock, and that's the last I see of her before we're back outside in the cool evening air.

"Very mature." Quinton laughs behind me.

"She deserved it." I try to justify my action.

Ren chooses to ignore the whole thing. "How did you get here?" he asks.

"Took my dad's driver. He is parked over there."

"Wanna ride back with us or in the boring car?" Quinton questions.

"What do you mean, ride back with you? How did you get here?"

Ren points at the two matt black motorcycles parked on the sidewalk a few feet from us. My mouth pops open. They came here with these? "Of course I want to ride with you!" I look up at Ren with the same puppy eyes I give my dad when I want something. "Please, can I ride with you?"

Ren gives me a knowing look, but I see the defeat in them immediately. "Fine, but you are wearing my helmet."

I almost squeal with excitement. Quinton goes over to talk to the driver while Ren takes me over to the motorcycles and grabs the helmet. He lets go of my hand to grab the helmet with both hands, bringing the straps to each side, he carefully places it over my head. It's a bit loose on my head, but Ren quickly fastens it with the chin straps.

Quinton joins us, putting his own helmet on while Ren goes without. I want to protest, but that would mean I wouldn't be able to ride with him since we only have two helmets, so I let it go.

Ren gets on the bike first, before motioning for me to sit behind him. I eagerly get on, scooting all the way toward him until my front is completely pressed against his back. I wrap my arms around his torso, interlacing my fingers.

"Don't let go," Ren warns before turning the key. The engine roars to life and the whole bike vibrates between my legs. Excitement fills my veins and everything about what happened inside the bar is now long forgotten.

Quinton pulls out in front of us, and Ren follows closely behind. We start off driving slow through downtown, but once we hit the interstate, Quinton and Ren get more daring. We weave in and out of traffic, gliding between cars like we're flying. I hold on to Ren like my life depends on it. And maybe it does, in more ways than one. Right now, I don't care. I just want to enjoy being this close to Ren, holding him while we're zooming through traffic, passing cars, and letting the wind rage around us.

27
REN

It's not a surprise when there's a soft knock at my bedroom door a couple of hours after we got back from the bar. I've been lying here, staring at the ceiling, thinking about Scarlet all this time. Remembering how good it was having her wrapped around me on the bike. There was a minute there where I wished I could keep going, like there was a way I could outrun everything. She has a way of making me believe shit like that is possible.

But I'm not a little kid anymore, and I wasn't that naïve even when I was a kid. Certain experiences have a way of beating the naïveté out of you.

"Yeah?" I ask, propping myself up on one elbow while the door opens, and Scarlet pokes her head into the room.

"Can I come in? I wanted to talk." I don't care what she wants to do. I wouldn't turn her down for anything. Especially when she's wearing a tiny pair of shorts and a thin T-shirt I can almost see through when the light from the hallway hits her from behind. I'm only human, and I've been missing her.

"Is it okay if I get in with you?" Rather than say anything, I throw the blanket back and lie down again before she climbs in next to me, burrowing under the blanket and curling up against my body. Fuck, she smells good. I can barely think for how good she smells. And how good it feels to have her next to me, so warm.

"Thanks." She clears her throat, itching a little closer. "Do you mind?" Her arm slides across my bare chest, and my breath catches. I'm not going to stop her from draping her arm over me, then resting her head on my chest. It's not long before she's in my arms, and I'm holding her close, grateful for the unexpected gift.

"I really needed this," she whispers. Her soft hair spills over my shoulder, and I take a deep breath to inhale the sweetness.

"I think I did, too," I admit. She makes a happy little noise that brings a smile to my lips before I tighten my grip around her. For a little while, it's enough to lie here in the dark, nobody watching my every move, nobody distrusting me. It's not long, though, until I have to ask the question that's been on my mind ever since I saw her tonight. "Tell me the truth. Why did you go to the bar?"

At first, she only grumbles a little, but I'm not going to let it go. I want to hear it from her mouth. She keeps talking about not taking risks anymore, then she does something like that. What if Tony hadn't been there?

Finally, she sighs. "You know I wanted to be there because you were there."

"Why?"

She raises her head and looks me in the eye, and in the faint moonlight coming in through the windows, I see the way she narrows her eyes. "What kind of question is that?"

"The kind of question I want an answer to."

"Very funny." She rests against my shoulder again with another sigh. "I just wanted to be with you. I mean, yeah, I wanted to make sure there weren't any stupid skanks trying to get in your pants, too. That was part of it."

The fact that she still wants to be with me after everything is enough as it is. But knowing she was jealous is a whole other story. This probably isn't the time for me to get all full of myself, but I can't help it. She really does still want me to the point of following me out to keep an eye on us.

Her leg slides over mine like she's trying to make herself more comfortable, and a helpless sort of yearning rises in me. I was staying away from her to keep her safe, but that doesn't mean I'm not still weak when it comes to her touch. Having her this close makes it tough to breathe, but I would rather suffocate than tell her to leave me alone. I need her too much.

"Can I ask you something?" It's not a comfortable question, but it's the question I keep coming back to every time I try to make sense of her having sex with River. All I want to know is why.

"Of course. Whatever you want to know." Fuck, she is so

sweet and trusting. Her heart is so open to me, even now. Just when I think I can't love her more, she proves otherwise.

Now that the moment is here, I have to find the right words. "When you're with River… having sex, I mean… is it different? Am I different?"

"That's really hard to explain," she murmurs in a soft voice.

"I shouldn't have asked."

"No, I'm glad you did. I'm just trying to find the words." She props her chin on her hand, sitting on my chest. All I can do is stroke her hair and try to commit the feel to my memory in case there's any reason we have to stay apart. Life is so damn unpredictable.

"When I'm with River," she eventually murmurs, speaking slowly, like she's choosing her words carefully, "you're… free. There's no restraint. You don't hold anything back. And I guess I like it." She squeezes her eyes tightly shut, wincing. "I'm sorry if that sounds wrong."

"I get it. So it's kind of wild and, I don't know, unpredictable?" I'm talking about what it's like when I fuck her, but I'm not the one actually doing it. Only I am. It's more confusing the more I try to make sense of it.

"It's like, rough and edgy. When you are River, you treat me like I can handle anything. There must be part of me that wants it that way. I don't know what it says about me," she admits.

I hate the way she sounds, like she's blaming herself somehow. It makes me hook a finger under her chin to lift her head so she's looking me in the eye. "God, you are beautiful," I whisper, since the sight of her overwhelming beauty wiped away what I was going to say. I have to concentrate to bring myself back into focus. "You're learning something about yourself. There's nothing wrong with that. And if I'm helping you figure it out, I guess that's good, too. You don't have anything to feel guilty about."

That earns me a scowl. "Don't say that. I know it's hard for you. I do feel like I have to apologize."

"I'm just saying there's nothing wrong with liking things a little different. Rougher and whatnot. There's nothing wrong with you. You're perfect."

"Okay, I don't know if I agree with all of that." Her teeth sink into her lip and something between us shifts. I can feel the change that comes over her before she asks, "Maybe I can make it up to you?"

"What do you mean?"

"Let me show you." The hand she was using to prop her chin on my chest now slides down the length of my abdomen. It's almost too much, the explosion of sensation that races through me because of her gentle touch. That's all it takes for my dick to go from twitching to swelling.

"What are you doing?" I know what she's doing, but it feels like I should say something as she wiggles her way down the bed and tugs at my pajama pants.

"Let me take care of you." All I can do is close my eyes and fall back against the pillow when she slides a hand under my waistband and wraps it around me. Her touch is soft and gentle, but it has the power to send heat spreading through me. There is no fighting her. I'm always going to need her like I need air or water. She's that necessary.

Right now, she's taking me into her mouth. Fuck, so good. My fists clench the sheets under me when her head starts to bob. The pressure from her mouth is insane, and it's not long before I lift my hips, feeding myself to her. "Yeah, that's it. Make me come for you," I rasp, my fingers buried in her soft hair while I move my hips. She's eager, slurping on me, moving faster. There's nothing in the world but this—the two of us in this bed. The way it's supposed to be, the way I want it always.

"Yes, Angel, you know what my cock likes," I whisper, and the little moan she releases in response is almost enough to make my eyes roll back. Everything about this is electric. I'm torn between wanting relief and hoping it never ends. I could spend the rest of my life suspended in total pleasure thanks to my angel's tongue running up and down my shaft before lapping at my head.

But it's still not enough. "Stop for a second." There's nothing I want less than losing the mind-blowing pressure of her mouth wrapped around me, but she deserves something, too. "I want you to sit on my face."

"What?" She's a little breathless from all that work. I hear the uncertainty in her voice even as I sit up and pull her closer. "What are you doing?"

"I need to taste that sweet pussy while I'm coming in your mouth. That's what I want." She shivers when I touch her cheek, then sighs softly. "Can you do that for me, Angel?"

She answers by pulling her T-shirt off all at once. I take a second to soak in the sight of her gorgeous tits before she wiggles out of her shorts. So eager, and all mine.

"Lie back," she whispers, and I'm not about to waste any time. My cock is dripping precum, and I'm as close to exploding as I've ever been, but the scent of her arousal once she settles over me kicks everything up to the next level. I don't even think about it before digging my fingers into her hips and pulling down hard, almost smothering myself in her wet, juicy folds.

"Oh, my god!" she whines, but anything else is stifled once she takes me in her mouth again. She sucks harder than before, almost like it's a contest to see who can make the other one come first. Right now, I'm in no hurry, driving my tongue deep into her cunt to lap up every drop of her sweetness, fucking her in time with her skillful strokes. She grinds hard against my face, using me, and I like that. It's what I want. I can give her everything River has. I need her to know that.

All either of us knows is how amazing this feels. She uses her hand on me when she comes up for air. "Yes, just like that," she begs, fucking me with her fist. "Make me come, Ren."

She's so close, and knowing she is gives me permission to stop fighting what's building in me. Her gasps for air have turned to high-pitched cries, which are muffled once she wraps her lips around me again. Yes, I'm going to come with her. I'm going to coat her throat the way her musky nectar coats my tongue.

By the time she goes stiff, I let go, and nothing has ever

felt so right as coming with her. We're both locked in this moment together, sharing something only we can.

And by the time she releases me and rolls away, her limp body tells me she's satisfied. I would ask her to check, but I'm too busy coming down from my high to say a word.

"Thank you for that." The bed shifts when Scarlet does, she swings around again so her head rests on my shoulder. She shivers against me, and I wrap my arms around her trembling form before pulling the blanket over her. This precious thing, the one good thing in my life. Somehow, she still trusts me. She still wants this with me. It's humbling in a way, maybe a little hard to understand. To her, I'm not a monster. I'm somebody worth being jealous over.

I still haven't made any sense of it by the time my eyes drift shut, and the sounds of her soft, gentle breathing lull me to sleep. For the first time in a long time, I'm peaceful and content. I only wish it could be like this always.

28
REN

"Full... so full..." Scarlet moans into the pillow.

I look down at her small body beneath me, her hands spreading her ass cheeks apart for me as I bury my cock inside her ass. "Good, I like you full of my cock. I like your holes good and stuffed. I'm gonna start fucking you, and you're going to be a good little girl and keep those ass cheeks spread for me." My voice is husky, almost unfamiliar, but it's definitely my own.

Scar keeps holding herself open for me as I move in and out of her ass at a steady pace. Fuck, she feels so incredibly tight.

"Fuck yes, that's it, slut, relax for me. Let me fuck you." At my crude words, she relaxes a little further, sinking into the mattress.

I increase my pace, fucking her faster and harder with each stroke. Part of me wonders if I'm hurting her, but the longer I go, the more she presses her ass up, urging me to go even deeper. She likes this.

"I'm going to fill your ass with my come, but I want you to come with me. I want you to fall apart while I fuck your ass," I say as I snake my arm around her until my fingers are right over her swollen clit. I rub the small bundle of nerves, roughly—rougher than I normally would—and it only takes a few seconds for her orgasm to sneak up on her.

"I—I'm coming..." She manages to spit out between choked moans.

A grunt rips from my throat, as I fuck her with deep strokes while pinching her clit so hard it must be painful. Her thighs quiver and her body tightens as her release takes hold of her.

"Fuck yes, milk my cock!" I roar as she comes all over my fingers.

"Ren!" Scarlet's sleepy voice drags me out of my dream. "Ren, wake up!"

My eyes fly open, and I'm greeted with the bright light of the bedside lamp. Scarlet is hovering over me, concern edged into her face. "I think you had a bad dream," she explains. Bad? I wouldn't say that. Disturbing. Maybe.

"What's wrong?" The concern grows in her voice.

"Nothing… I think… I wasn't dreaming. It felt more like I was remembering something. River's memory."

Scarlet swallows slowly, her delicate throat moving. "What kind of memory?" She still sound worried, but this time for a different reason.

"I was fucking your ass. On this bed. You were spreading your cheeks for me, and I called you slut, and my good little girl."

Scarlet's eyes go wide, her whole face turns a hue of pink. I know I'm right before she says the words. This was a memory. This really happened. I did that to her… and she liked it.

"It's true. You did that… we did that," she tells me shyly.

"And you enjoyed it very much," I point out, still shocked by the revelation.

"Did you not?" Scarlet questions.

"I did." Fuck me, I did. It was so fucking hot having her ass wrapped around my cock. Squeezing me so tightly. "I just didn't expect you to like it that much."

"Are you disappointed in me?"

Disappointed? "What?! No! Why would you say that?"

"Because you call me your angel and now you know that there is a depraved part of me that likes to be called names during sex."

"Oh, Scarlet." I sit up straight, bringing my hand up to cup her cheek. I look deep into her eyes when I speak the next words. "There is nothing you could say or do that would make me stop loving you or think badly of you in any way. I don't care what you like in bed as long as you share it with me."

Relief washes over her features before excitement takes hold of her. "Ren, do you realize what just happened? You remembered what you did as River. That's a great step forward."

"It is," I agree, wishing I could access those memories as I please. Especially the explicit ones. "What time is it?"

Scarlet checks her phone on the nightstand. "Seven in the morning."

"I don't think I can go back to sleep now. I'm going to head in the shower."

"I'll join you!" Scarlet gets up from the bed eagerly, heading straight for the attached bathroom. I follow close behind, watching her remove the shirt and panties she is wearing until she is completely bare to me.

My cock roars to life. Even though I came inside her mouth just a few hours ago, I'm ready to devour her all over again. I peel my shorts off and turn on the hot water in my shower. Not waiting till it gets warm, I step under the cold spray to cool off. The icy water hits my heated skin, and my dick immediately deflates.

"I don't know how you stand cold showers, I'd die," Scarlet says, rubbing her hands over her arms to warm up.

"You get used to it." I grin at her. "It's getting warm now, you can come in without freezing to death."

"Thank god!" Scarlet slips under the shower, her silky skin brushing against mine in the process. I stifle a moan. I never get over the effect this woman has on me. One touch is all it takes for me to want her all over again.

She starts to wash her hair, and I get a soapy washcloth and wash the rest of her body. When I'm done with her, we switch. Now she is washing me, and I thoroughly enjoy every second of it.

"If I didn't have an appointment with Dr. Stone, I would fuck you against this wall right now."

"Maybe we need another shower later then," Scarlet teases.

"Not maybe, definitely." I give her a little slap on the ass, making her squeal in surprise before she breaks out giggling, a sound that warms my chest.

Once we're both clean from top to bottom, we get out of the shower and dry off. I wrap Scarlet in a white fluffy towel, loving the way she lets me take care of her. After we're dry, I get dressed, while Scarlet blow dries her hair in the bathroom.

Again, a sense of normality hits me. This is my life now, I realize. I have everything I ever wanted. Scarlet and my family by my side, and Rebecca dead. I just wish I could let New Haven go. I know I have to. It's the only way I can keep the rest.

I check the time on the clock next to my bed. "The doctor will be here any minute now," I yell into the bathroom.

Scarlet rushes out to get dressed, and I can't help watching every move she makes. No matter what she does, she looks beautiful and irresistible. She puts her uncombed hair into a messy bun and slips her sneakers on her feet.

"Ready," she announces.

Together, we walk downstairs, where Dr. Stone is already ringing the doorbell. "Perfect timing," I point out.

Scarlet rushes to the door to let the doctor in. "Hello, Scarlet. Hello, Ren?" She says my name as a question.

"Yes, it's me today," I confirm, making her smile and nod. I can't help but wonder if she would have the same expression for River. Shaking the thought away, I walk the doctor and Scarlet over to the sitting area we have been conducting our sessions the last few times. Dr. Stone sits down on a single chair, getting out her notebook and pencil while Scar and I take one of the couches.

Most times, it is just Dr. Stone and me, but sometimes, Scarlet likes to sit in, which we all agree is not a bad thing. She needs to know everything I know since she has to deal with me.

"How have you been, Ren?"

"Great, I had a dream today… but it was really a memory—River's memory, Scarlet confirmed."

"Oh, that's wonderful, Ren. That's exactly what we have been working toward. You and River need to mentally connect so you can live in harmony. What was the memory about?"

I clear my throat, moving my gaze from the doctor to Scarlet. Only when Scar gives me a tiny nod, do I talk. "It was a memory of me as River having sex with Scarlet."

If Dr. Stone is shocked, she doesn't let it show. "And how did that make you feel?"

I take a few seconds to think about it before I answer. "Relieved, and maybe a little content. Before, it was hard for me to wrap my mind around not remembering. It felt like River was a different person, but now that I've had this memory come back, it's different. Now I know it was still me."

"Excellent. That is very good progress, Ren. Much faster than other patients I've worked with. You should be proud of yourself and all the work you have put in."

"Thank you for saying that."

"Does that mean this will happen more often now? Ren remembering, I mean?" Scarlet asks.

"Hopefully, yes. This is definitely a good start." Dr. Stone turns to me. "If you are up for it, I would like to try a little exercise today that might help you to connect with River more."

"I'm up for anything," I say with confidence.

"All right, for this exercise, I need you to lie down and get comfortable."

"Okay." I nod and kick off my shoes. Shifting my body, I lie down on the couch and prop my head on Scarlet' lap. "I'm comfortable."

"Close your eyes and take a few calming breaths," Dr. Stone says before coaching me through some breathing exercises. At the end of it, I feel more than relaxed, almost lightheaded. My mind has drifted to a calming place of darkness.

"Now I want you to imagine a red door in front of you. Do you see it?"

I do what she asks and imagine a red door appearing in my mind. "Yes, I see it."

"I want you to reach for it, grab the doorknob, and turn it. Open the door and behind the door you see River."

Again, I do as she asks. I reach for the doorknob and open the door, pushing it open until I see River on the other side. I used to see him in my head all the time, hallucinating, FaceTime, timing and talking on the phone, but since the doctor started me on medication, those hallucinations have become nonexciting.

"Do you see him?" The doctor questions.

"Yes."

"Good. Now tell him what you would usually write in your notebook. Tell him how you feel and what you want him to do."

"I just want him to be happy, or at least content with what we accomplished. Rebecca is dead and so is her son. We're alive and have been forgiven by the people who we love the most. That needs to be enough."

It will never be enough. River tells me in my mind.

"It has to be," I add. "I'll do whatever it takes to make you understand." Because that's the only chance I have for a happy ending.

29
SCARLET

There is nothing like waking up next to the man I love. It's something so simple, and I'd bet so many people take it for granted. It's easy to do when you've never seen the way everything can change in an instance. It's easy to lose sight of everything that could go wrong.

But nothing is wrong now. Ren is getting better every day, and he's not afraid to have me around him anymore. I stretch with a smile, throwing my arms over my head and even groaning happily. There is nothing in the world like a good stretch after a long night's sleep.

I am about to announce this to Ren before my eyes open, and I find myself alone.

All the warmth and happiness I just soaked in turns icy cold. "Ren?" I whisper, my heart in my throat. When nothing greets me but silence, I scramble out of the bed, pulling on the jeans and tee I left on the floor last night before crawling in next to him. What if he turned into River and is walking around the house, wanting to hurt somebody? Is there ever going to be a time when I don't fear that? Once I'm dressed, I race for the door and fling it open.

And jump back, yelping in surprise to see Ren standing on the other side. From the looks of it, he was about to reach for the doorknob to come inside. He jumps a little, too, and we have one of those moments where we both stand around with our hands on our chest, catching our breath and laughing.

"Sorry." He chuckles, wincing. "I didn't mean to scare you."

"It's okay." More than okay. All of my fears dissolve when I find him smiling, looking like the Ren I fell in love with. "I woke up, and you weren't here, and I didn't know what to think."

"Oh, that. I was coming in to tell you everything's set up."

Suspicion winds its way through me. "What do you mean, everything?"

"Come see." He holds out his hand. I don't have to think twice before taking it and following him downstairs, even if I'm not quite sure what is happening. But this is Ren, and I trust Ren, and besides, we're in my family's house. There are guards everywhere.

It's a balmy, beautiful morning, with a warm breeze that stirs my hair once we step out onto the terrace. Ren has set up breakfast for us at one of the tables by the railing leading to the garden. "Sort of like a date, right?" he asks, pulling me close for a sweet kiss. I love the way he smiles down at me. Sort of boyish, proud of himself for surprising me.

"This is amazing," I tell him, beaming as I look over the table full of food. The scent of cinnamon and sugar makes my mouth water, something that only gets worse when he lifts the lid off a platter full of bacon. "Oh, my god, I need that."

"Wow. I didn't know you'd get this excited." He chuckles as he pulls a chair out for me to take a seat. "There's orange juice, coffee, French toast and potatoes, too."

"And you," I remind him, taking him by the shirt and pulling him down for another passionate kiss before he sits across from me. "Thank you. This is so thoughtful."

"It's nothing. I can't wait to take you out for real." There's a little bit of wistfulness in his voice, and I hate to hear it. I don't want anything to ruin this wonderful morning together.

"I'm just happy to be here with you." And to see him looking so good and so happy. So much like himself. It's been days since I last saw River. I can tell he's relieved by that. It makes him feel more confident. Like he's not always waiting for something bad to happen.

I can breathe a little easier, too. It's almost possible to believe we're going to have a happy ending after everything we've been through.

"I didn't realize I was this hungry," he mumbles around a mouthful of food. I don't think I've ever seen him shove it in like that. Another thing to be happy about, watching him enjoy himself. I am, too, already eyeing a third slice of French toast when I've barely finished the first two.

"That's how it goes. You take a bite of something delicious, and all of a sudden, you need more." I smirk, wondering if he'll catch my meaning.

"Yeah, that sounds familiar." Something wicked flashes in his eyes when they meet mine. "I shouldn't be so surprised I'm this hungry after the appetite I worked up overnight."

That's all it takes for a delicious little shiver to run down my spine. Maybe he's trying to prove himself after what I confessed a few days back about how it feels to be with River. I don't know. I only know there's something wild in him now. Like he was holding back before but understands he doesn't have to anymore. Like that part of him was always inside—which it must've been, if it manifested in the form of River—only now he can let it out and be his entire self. I guess if nothing else good comes out of all of this, we have that much.

"Any plans for the day?" he asks me. We're just two normal people in love, eating breakfast together. I could get used to this.

Shrugging, I offer, "I'm not sure. I might help Aspen out with some nursery stuff."

He must figure out right away what's going on in my head since his face falls. "You're still sad about the baby."

"How can I be when there was never a baby in the first place?" But, yes, that's why the idea of spending an afternoon with my sister-in-law stings a lot. It's sort of exhausting, having to put on a happy face and pretend everything's cool when inside all I can do is wonder when it's going to be my turn. I hate myself for thinking that way. It's immature, for one thing, and for another, Aspen would never think that way if our positions were reversed. She is much too sweet and generous for that, while I'm just being selfish.

"You're entitled to feel how you feel," he reminds me in a soft but firm voice. "Don't be so hard on yourself."

"I know you're right." And I love him even more for hearing me out and not trying to gloss over my feelings. Growing up with a father like mine, I'm used to people thinking they can solve all my problems for me. He's not trying to do that. He just wants to help me through it. He is exactly what I need, perfect for me in every way.

"What are you smiling about?" He's smiling, too, when I look up from my orange juice.

"Probably about how much I love you." We both lean across the table for a kiss. He tastes like syrup and bacon and orange juice, and I drink him in, catching up for lost time.

That is, until my stomach turns out of nowhere. "Oh, shit." I sit back in my chair, one hand on my belly while the other creeps up over my mouth. "I don't feel so good. I think I ate too fast."

"What's wrong?"

I don't have time to answer. There's only enough time for me to catch sight of his worried expression before I make a run for it, tearing into the house and through the kitchen. It's a miracle I make it to the powder room in time, throwing myself on the floor in front of the toilet not a split second before everything I just ate comes back up in a painful rush. My stomach keeps cramping and wave after wave splashes into the bowl. There's nothing for me to do but wait for it to pass, and by the time it does, my ribs ache from the force of gagging that hard.

At some point, Ren must have followed me, and now he's holding my hair back with one hand while rubbing my back with the other. "I'm sorry. Did you already feel sick? You didn't need to eat with me if you felt sick, you know."

"But I didn't." I'm pretty sure it's over now, so I flush the toilet before closing the lid and resting my forehead against the cool wood. "I felt fine until, like, thirty seconds ago."

The slow, rhythmic motion from his hand ceases. "When was the last time you had a period?"

That's a good question. I honestly can't remember. It's enough to make me open my eyes and sit up, forgetting the lingering nausea for a second while I think back. "Everything is such a blur. It's hard for me to remember what happened when."

"You get what I'm asking, right? Are you sure you're not pregnant?"

"The test was negative," I remind him with a shrug. "So it's not that."

His troubled eyes narrow. "Are those tests always right?"

Honestly, I have no idea. "Well, either way, it's been a long time since my last period. Maybe I should go to the doctor."

"I want to go with you." It comes out all at once, almost a single word. "There's still a chance you're pregnant. The test could've been wrong. I want to be there with you."

And I want nothing more in the whole world than to have him by my side. He'll never know how much it means to hear that. It gives me the courage to stand on my feet and, after running up to get changed and brush my teeth, head down to Dad's office. I still feel a little queasy, but I'm pretty sure I vomited up every ounce of what was in my stomach.

Could I be pregnant? The possibility makes my pulse race as I approach the open door. Good. He's not busy. He might be in a decent mood.

And he seems to be, giving me his full attention when I walk in instead of only glancing my way before going back to his work. "Good morning. You look a little green. Are you feeling all right?"

It's not like him to be that observant, which tells me I must look like hell. But right now, it feels like that's a good thing. "Have a big favor to ask you."

Groaning, he says, "Exactly what a father wants to hear first thing in the morning."

"It's not a big deal or anything. But I need to make an appointment with the doctor."

"Are you sick? Is there something you're not telling me?" He's already halfway out of his chair, looking either ready to kill somebody or buy a new hospital wing to make sure I'm taken care of.

"I'm not sick. But…" I mean, I don't want to lie. And considering I'm about to ask permission to take Ren with me, he needs to understand the subtext here. Why this is so important. "Don't freak out. I thought I might be for a little while, but I took a test, and it said I wasn't. But I just got sick out of nowhere, and… I don't want to get too personal, but…" All the words come rushing out at once. I don't even think they make sense or explain what is going on. Thankfully, Dad helps me out.

He holds up a hand, sinking back into his chair with a thump. "Are you telling me what I think you're telling me?"

"I might be pregnant," I whisper, trembling. "It would've happened when we were at that cabin. I swear, I wasn't trying to keep a secret. I really didn't think I was. But maybe I should go. And I want him to go with me. He has the right to be there if it turns out I really am pregnant."

He closes his eyes, rubbing his temples in circles. I know better than to push my luck, so I stand here and wait for him to speak instead of demanding he give me an answer right away. "Obviously, this is not the time to go into specifics of what this could mean," Dad murmurs. "What matters now is getting you the care you may need. And I have to agree with you. If you are going to have a baby, Ren deserves to be there with you. That is why he'll go with you, but you'll have two guards. No arguments."

"I'm not arguing." Honestly, I didn't expect him to give in that easily. I'm already calling the gynecologist before I've left the room, and soon Ren and I are sitting in the backseat of an SUV, holding hands, both of us too nervous to say much of anything. But it's a good kind of nerves. I can feel it. I can see it in the way he smiles whenever I catch his eye. I was so scared about how he would react when he found out, wasn't I? But he's come such a long way since we came back, too.

I'm sure the doctor has seen plenty of girls like me: young, a little scared, completely clueless. All it takes is me peeing in a cup, which I hand over to one of the nurses before heading back into the exam room where Ren is waiting. He offers a hopeful little smile that reminds me everything's going to be okay, no matter what the result is. I know I have him. That's all I've ever wanted.

Still, my heart catches, and I forget to breathe when the door opens, and the doctor steps in. "Scarlet, the test came back positive. You're pregnant."

It's like the world stops turning for a second. I'm pregnant. I'm really pregnant, the doctor said so. "Oh, my god." There are tears in my eyes when I turn to Ren, whose mouth is hanging open. He must see how anxious I am to hear his feelings because he is quick to pull me close for a tight hug. He's happy. *Oh, thank you, God.*

After a brief exam, I lie back on the table while she pulls out the ultrasound equipment. It seems like everything's happening so fast—just a couple of hours ago I woke up thinking this was an ordinary day. Now, there's gel being squirted on my stomach so the three of us can get a look at what's growing inside me. Our baby.

"There we are." The doctor is smiling from ear to ear as she moves the wand over my stomach. "There's your baby. Hear the heartbeat?" For a second there, I thought it was my own heart I was hearing.

All I can do is stare at the screen in wonder with Ren's hand clutching mine while the doctor taps a keyboard and takes notes. "Based on the measurements here, it looks like you're around nine weeks along. Still plenty of time to go, but you and baby seem healthy. Congratulations."

Finally, I'm able to tear my gaze away from the image on the screen so I can look at Ren. He's still staring, his face full of wonder as he gazes at what we created together.

"Congratulations," I whisper, squeezing his hand.

All he does is beam and release a tiny laugh. It's the happiest I've ever heard him.

30
REN

"So, how are we feeling today?" Dr. Stone folds her hands in her lap and wears a knowing smile. I still get the feeling she knows more about me than I do. Even after all these weeks of sitting with her and opening myself up, I haven't gotten used to it.

"Pretty much the same as our last session." It amazes me that I don't feel threatened anymore. I did for so long, nervous and afraid to share secrets I held inside for years. Now it's like we're having a normal conversation. Just two people sitting around, shooting the shit. It just so happens one of us is being paid for it.

"Any visits from River lately?"

I hold up one finger, and as stupid as it is, I feel a little proud. "It wasn't bad. I think I was overwhelmed at the time. It didn't last long—according to Scarlet, anyway. She said he was there, then he was gone. I barely noticed any time passed."

"What were you overwhelmed about? What set it off?"

The fact that she has to ask leaves me laughing a little. "I mean, do I need anything else? I'm gonna be a father."

Her head tips to the side. "I thought you were happy about that?"

"I am," I tell her right away. There shouldn't be any doubt about that. "But it's a lot. It's overwhelming."

"But not in a bad way?"

Shaking my head, I tell her, "Oh, no. Not in a bad way at all. I mean, it's not like I planned this. It's not the kind of thing you grow up imagining happening. But it's a good thing. It's really good."

She sighs like she's relieved. "That's wonderful. I'm happy for both of you. This is a nice, fresh beginning. New life."

I know what she's saying. I completely agree. But… "I wonder if I can be a good parent after everything I went through."

"You've never had anything but positive things to say about Sophie and Roman. Have you been holding something back?"

I see where she's going with this, and I have to laugh softly at myself when I look at it that way. "No, they're great. They did more for me and Luna than they had to, for sure."

"That's what parents do. That's what you're going to do for your child. Focus on those good things we've talked about. Use the techniques we've developed to work through those moments of uncertainty when you're feeling the most agitated or confused."

That's what's been getting me through lately. "Right. Thank you. I just needed to talk it out, I guess."

"How far along is Scarlet now?"

"Twelve weeks. First trimester over, and she was hardly aware."

The doctor chuckles softly. "Lucky girl. Everything's going well?"

"Sure. She's great. Her parents... Xander's not throwing a party or anything, but he's not threatening to kill me, either."

Her lips twitch. "That's a very good start."

And it is. Finally, I have a new start. No more hiding secrets in the shadows, no more living in darkness. No more being afraid to reach out for the light, because now I know there's someone there who will take my hand. There's no flailing around, lost and confused. I know who I am and where I want to be.

Once our session is over, I turn my thoughts to something that's been on my mind for weeks. Each day that passes takes us one day closer to the baby being born. There are some decisions to be made, big ones. If this is really going to be a new start, it means going into it with a clean slate.

Can I do that? Can I live with knowing New Haven still exists? I might have to. Rebecca is gone. If I go in there with guns blazing, all alone—which I would be, since Xander has already refused to get involved with the Russians—what would come out of it besides my death? It would mean my baby being raised without a father. I wouldn't do that to them, and I sure as hell wouldn't do it to Scarlet.

I love her enough and love our unborn child enough to make the decision to let go. I can't save the world. I need to put this behind me once and for all, which means accepting the things I can't change. Isn't that part of the serenity prayer? Serenity has never been something I've strived for, but I'm starting to understand it might not be such a bad idea. I can't live the rest of my life full of hate, craving vengeance. It's time for something new and better.

Which is why, even though my heart is banging against my ribs like a drum, and my knees are shaking a hell of a lot harder than I would ever admit to anyone, I leave my room and head downstairs, where I know I'll find Xander. I wouldn't be surprised if he slept in his office, he spends so much time in there. There's something almost comforting about it, though. Knowing what to expect.

His brows lift when I knock. "How did it go with the doctor?"

"It went well. I get the feeling she's ready to be done with me."

Sitting back in his chair, he nods, gesturing for me to have a seat before I have the chance to ask if I can take it. I wonder if he would be so generous if he knew why I'm paying this visit. "You've improved greatly. It makes sense your sessions would become fewer and further between. I'm sure she'll want to follow up with you from time to time—it might be a good idea to advocate for that. Just to be sure things are still going smoothly. I know it's been hard work, and I give you a great deal of credit."

As much as I love hearing this and appreciate it, I also wish he wouldn't say it. His whole attitude is going to change in about five seconds. "There's something I wanted to talk to you about," I begin after clearing my throat. Why is this so hard? Oh, right, because it's probably the most important decision I've ever made, and my entire life hangs in the balance. No big deal.

"Go ahead. What's on your mind?"

I find it hard to believe he doesn't at least have a clue, but then he might want to let me dangle a little rather than make this easy on me. It's sort of a father's prerogative, I guess. "I'm just going to say it flat-out. I want to ask Scarlet to marry me. But first, I wanted to get your blessing."

I'm only trying to do the right thing. I mean, I would've asked her to marry me anyway. That's always been in my heart. It just so happened a bunch of other shit got in the way.

Now, with the baby, it seems more important than ever to make us a real, solid family. I want to do right by her. I want to be able to protect her and the baby. And I want to say all of that, I do, but something about Xander's penetrative stare makes it hard to put the feelings into words. I can't help thinking it would all sound hopelessly pathetic if I tried to explain what I'm thinking. Xander is not the guy who talks about feelings—neither am I, for that matter.

Besides, why would I bother struggling to find the words when I'm sure he'll cut me off and throw me out of his house for good? It has to be what's on his mind as he sits there staring at me from the other side of the enormous desk between us. I'm pretty sure he doesn't blink. What did I expect? For him to welcome me into the family with open arms?

His eyes close. He takes a deep breath. I'm about to get my ass handed to me. Good thing Scarlet is worth it.

The man keeps me waiting for much too long before, finally, a slow smile tugs at the corners of his mouth. "It's about time."

I can't believe my ears any more than I believe what my eyes are telling me. He actually looks happy. "Seriously? You mean that?"

"It's a shame you got things a little backward, is all." When I give him a confused look, he explains, "You're supposed to get married before you knock my daughter up, Ren. But I suppose I can forgive you."

"I CAN'T WAIT to bring the baby out here." Scarlet's arm is wrapped around mine, her head leaning against my shoulder while we walk through the garden. The aroma of new spring flowers perfumes the breeze. In a few months, the air will be thick with bees and butterflies and so much color will spread across the grounds. I like the idea of bringing the baby out here, too.

The sun is warm on my neck and shoulders, and there's a sweet breeze stirring Scarlet's hair and the long, flowing dress she wears. It's the kind of perfect day that gives a person hope. It's always so much easier to have hope on a day like this. "How are you feeling?" I ask her.

"Same as I was the last time you asked me that question." There's a lot of love in her voice. She looks up at me, grinning. "I feel great. I really do. I didn't think I could ever be this happy."

Still, her footsteps falter after a while, and I know why. There's a lot I don't remember, a lot of bits and pieces banging around inside my skull. But I remember taking her from this place. Out here in the garden, where we wrestled in the mud while the rain beat down on us and thunder and lightning crackled through the air. On a day like this, it's hard to believe that night ever took place.

"What is that over there?" I slow my pace, gravel crunching under my shoes, while I point toward a hedge of roses whose buds are just beginning to develop.

"What's what?" Scarlet releases my arm and takes a few steps toward the hedge.

"There's something there. Is it paper?"

"I think it is." She snatches the folded paper out of the crisscrossing stems, unfolding it slowly. I have to take a second to admire how beautiful she is right now. With the sun shining on her hair, painting her skin golden. She is truly an angel placed on earth just for me.

"I stole you from this place once," she murmurs, reading the message printed on the paper. "But you stole my heart long before that."

By the time she turns, eyes wide and full of questions, I'm on one knee. It makes her fall back a step with a hand against her chest, and a disbelieving laugh bursts out of her before she asks, "What is this? Is this real?"

"It's real." Just as real as the box in my back pocket, which I now pull out. Mom practically insisted on giving me a ring that's been in the family for years, and I open the box to present it to Scarlet. My angel. "You're all I'll ever want. Your happiness, your safety, that's what my life is all about now. Please, tell me you'll let me spend the rest of my life devoted to nothing more than you and our family. I can't promise I'm always going to make it easy for you, but I will always love you with everything in me. Do you think you could take a chance and become my wife?"

The thing is, she doesn't even look at the ring. She's too busy staring at me, hands covering her mouth, her eyes filling with tears. Happy tears? I sure as hell hope so. I've never understood until this very moment what it means to have my life completely in somebody else's hands. My future, all of me, it's all wrapped up in her.

"Of course I will," she squeaks out, head bobbing up and down. The sun that already shone so bright is now dazzling as I stand and hold out my arms for her to throw herself into them. I'm holding the entire world now, everything that matters most. I'm never letting go.

"I love you." She takes my face in her hands, beaming up at me before our mouths meet in the sweetest, most tender kiss. The sort of kiss that marks new beginnings. Her tears wet my cheeks by the time she pulls back, laughing and crying all at once. "I love you so much. I can't believe this. We're getting married."

Taking her left hand, I slide the four-carat diamond solitaire over her ring finger. "It's official now. No turning back."

"As if I want to."

After taking a second to admire the platinum band, she takes me by the back of the neck with that hand and pulls me in for another kiss.

EPILOGUE

Scarlet

One Year Later

I can hardly believe it. A year ago, this day seemed so far off. Like it would never get here. More of a concept than anything else. Something I looked forward to every day, even while I was looking forward to the baby's arrival. It's been a year full of hope and joy and love, and it's been better than anything I ever imagined, even in my most childish fantasies. Back when the closest I could get to Ren was in a dream.

This is no dream. Standing here, just inside the doorway,

leading out to the garden, everything is very real. I see it all so clearly. The sky is bluer than I've ever seen it, the trees greener, the flowers more lush and vibrant. Their sweetness drifts my way through the open door, and I close my eyes, trying to take it all in. I want to absorb this moment. Standing here, minutes away from my biggest dream coming true.

Everyone is already out there. From where I stand, I hear Rose babbling happily in Mom's arms. My little girl. Just the thought of her makes my heart swell. I didn't know it was possible to love the way I love her. I have everything I've ever dreamed of.

Well, not quite yet. In a few minutes, I will. Once Dad walks me down the aisle.

He's wearing a gentle smile as he approaches, looking me up and down. "You look radiant," he tells me as he admires my ivory lace gown. I wanted something soft and romantic to suit the setting, and the long skirt swishes gently around my legs when I turn in place for him.

"Thank you," I whisper, already fighting back the waves of emotion that have been trying to drown me all day. "Thank you for all of this. None of it would be possible without you."

"It's a father's privilege to give his daughter a beautiful wedding." He gently kisses my cheek, chuckling. "Don't want to ruin your makeup. Your mother made me promise."

Obviously, he didn't really mean his promise, because he adds, "You've been a wonderful daughter and have always given your mother and me a lot of happiness. Now that I've watched you grow into the role of mother, I couldn't be more proud of the woman you've become."

"So much for my makeup." I laugh through the tears I can't hold back. He takes a handkerchief from his breast pocket and dabs the corners of my eyes while we laugh together.

"And now, there's a very anxious young man waiting for you at the far end of the garden. Do you think we should go out and meet him?" I answer by taking his offered arm, a bouquet of lush gardenias in my other hand.

Luna and Aspen take that as their cue, both of them giving me big smiles before turning to face the guests. Once Luna takes her first step onto the white runner, a string quartet begins playing Canon in D. The guests waiting in the rows of white chairs turn to watch the girls float down the aisle, their rose-pink dresses matching the roses pinned in their hair and the delicate blooms dotting the hedges. Once they reach the end of the runner, it's our turn.

Please, don't let me forget a second of this. The smiling faces of so many people I love. Sophie and Roman, both looking choked up on their side of the aisle. Mom, holding Rose in one arm and clutching little Tristen's hand to keep him in place. His blue suit matches the ones worn by his daddy and Ren, and Tristen might be the cutest thing I've ever seen. He and Rose are already joined at the hip, and I hope they grow up with a strong bond. If the past couple of years have taught me anything, it's the importance of family.

Mom is sniffling through her bright smile. Rose waves both arms when she recognizes her mommy walking slowly toward her—I blow her a kiss, then another for Mom. I couldn't have done any of this without her support.

At the end of the runner stands my brother, hands folded in front of him, smiling at me before grinning at his best friend. The two of them managed to get past everything that took place when Ren was at the height of his illness. Seeing them together again, the way they used to be, has been one of the most satisfying parts of the past year, right up there with Rose's birth, as far as I'm concerned. I want Ren to have everything he needs, and the best friend who has always been more like a brother to him is definitely one of those things.

Finally, my gaze lands on the man I'm about to marry. I can't breathe when our eyes meet, and he flashes the sort of smile that still makes butterflies flutter in my stomach. He is so handsome in his navy suit, but it's the love radiating from his face that makes him the most beautiful thing I've ever seen. That's the only word I can think of to describe him now. The past year has only made him more precious to me. Watching him become a father, seeing the gentle part of his soul coming to the surface whenever he plays with Rose or rocks her to sleep.

He blows out a soft whistle when I join him. "You are stunning," he whispers, then shakes Dad's hand before taking mine. Luna holds my bouquet before I turn to her brother. I have never felt so sure of anything in my life as I do at this very moment.

The officiant smiles at both of us before looking out over the gathering of family and friends. "Dearly beloved, we are here today to join Scarlet and Ren in matrimony. It is my honor and privilege to stand before you and assist in this process, but it is the love and devotion these two share that makes this possible."

Now I am so glad we decided not to write our own vows, because I'm pretty sure I couldn't make it through the first sentence without bawling my eyes out. I can barely hold back the tears as I look up into the shining eyes of the love of my life. He has given me everything I've ever wanted, and even more that I never knew I needed.

But if I did write my own vows, I would have to tell him how grateful I am for him working so hard to get better for both of us. I would tell him how proud I am of how far he's come and how he has changed my entire life for the better in a hundred little ways. How every day, he finds a way to make me love him more. I wouldn't think it was possible, but there's no denying facts. And the fact is, I love him more at this moment than I did during our rehearsal dinner last night.

The titanium band fits his finger perfectly. "With this ring, I thee wed," I manage to choke out without blubbering. Mom sobs softly, and I glance over to find Dad wrapping his free arm around her while holding Tristen in the other.

By the time Ren slides the diamond-encrusted platinum band over my finger, I can't possibly hold back anymore. The first tears start to fall. He reaches out to brush one of them away from my cheek, and I'm pretty sure I hear Aspen swooning behind me.

The officiant places a hand on my shoulder and the other

on Ren's, raising his voice to make the big announcement we've all been waiting to hear. "By the power vested in me, I declare them husband and wife." There's barely time for me to catch my breath before Ren takes me in his arms to seal the first moment of our new life with a passionate kiss I wish could last forever.

Just like that, I'm a wife. He is my husband. And this is only the beginning.

Sitting in the back of an SUV when I ought to be getting ready to celebrate my wedding night, only one thing is on my mind: this had better be good.

The last thing I feel like doing after hours of dancing and celebrating is being driven out to the middle of nowhere with Ren, our dads, and Quinton. Ren seems as confused as I am, sitting by my side with his tie loosened and the top button of his shirt open. They didn't even give us time to get changed after the reception before telling us there was a wedding gift waiting. I look at him, lifting my brows, and all he can do is shrug.

"We'll be there soon," Q assures us from his position on Ren's right side. I watch him tap his fingers against his knee, which bounces rhythmically like he's on edge. Come to think of it, he's been a little weird lately. So has Dad, now that I think about it. I was willing to brush it aside in the last days of wedding planning, but now it's blatantly obvious they've been up to something. If they didn't seem so twitchy, I might think it's something good and positive.

Finally, it's clear where we're heading. I remember this route. So does Ren—slowly, his posture stiffens, and his hand clamps a little tighter around mine. "Why are you taking us there?" he asks in a flat voice. There's no need to say the name. I wouldn't mind if I never heard it again, frankly.

"You'll see soon enough," Dad tells him. He and Roman sit in a pair of seats in front of us with a bodyguard and driver in the front row. I watch as they exchange a look and wonder why the hell they brought a guard along.

The only thing to light the area around us is the stars twinkling overhead by the time we come to a stop on the side of an otherwise empty road. My stomach turns as amber lights glow in the distance, maybe half a mile or so from where we've parked. Dad and Roman exchange another look, and Roman nods before reaching under his seat, pulling out a nondescript, plain wooden box. "Open it," he murmurs, handing it to Ren.

I watch with my heart in my throat, wondering what's beneath the hinged lid. The only thing in there is a small device with a button on top. "What is this?" Ren asks, looking around. He even looks at me, like I would have the first idea. I'm as clueless as he is.

"Consider it a wedding gift to both of you." Dad nods toward the device. "Push that button, and it's all over."

I think I'm starting to get the idea, and it fills me with a mix of surprise and concern. I mean, this is pretty extreme. "What about the people inside?" I ask, chewing my lip and looking out the window. I've been there. I've seen them, or at least some of them. They're as innocent as Ren ever was, for the most part. Sure, some of them are probably too twisted and brainwashed to be considered innocent anymore, but mostly, the people there are trapped.

"Don't worry about that." Q's voice is tight, sharp. "They've been evacuated. The innocents, anyway." So that's what they've been up to. They've been arranging this all along, working behind the scenes.

"So, what you're saying is this would destroy the compound?" Ren's expression reminds me of the way he looked when we first saw Rose on that ultrasound. He's full of wonder and disbelief, standing at a threshold of something he has wanted for years. He's about to get everything he dreamed of.

"How long have you been planning this?" Because I need to know. This isn't the kind of thing they could've done overnight. How much have I missed while I was knee-deep in wedding planning?

Roman chuckles, exchanging a glance with Dad and Q. "It's been in the works for quite some time."

"But I thought..." Ren's gaze lands on Dad, who nods in understanding. "You said..."

"Yes, I know," Dad admits. "After giving it some thought and planning, we devised this solution. If I were you, I'd get it over with quickly."

"You deserve a new start, Son," Roman concludes. "It's time to shut the door on this part of your life and move forward."

"We wanted to be sure none of this would ever hang over your head," Q explains. "Once and for all, let's put an end to it."

Ren releases a shaky breath, his eyes glued to the device. "I never thought I would get this chance," he murmurs. "I told myself to let it go."

My heart skips a beat when he hovers his finger over the button. "Fuck it."

It happens so fast. He jams his finger against the button and within moments, the first explosion lights the night sky. It sets off a chain reaction, one fireball after another exploding into the darkness. It's so intense, the ground shakes at a distance.

The glow plays off Ren's profile, his face immobile as he watches the destruction unfold. I tuck my hand in his elbow and lean against him, whispering, "It's over. It's all over. And they're never going to hurt anybody again."

He releases a deep breath before nodding firmly. It's the closing of one door and the opening of another. "Let's go home."

Soon, we're turning around, leaving everything behind us once and for all. We're finally free.

My family, my husband, and me.

Thank you for reading Touch of Chaos. If you haven't read about Aspen and Quinton, you can find their story in King of Corium.

ABOUT THE C. HALLMAN

C. Hallman is a *USA Today* Bestselling Author who wrote her debut novel in 2018 and has since published over 100 books in various romance subgenres. Her works have been on numerous bestseller lists and have been translated into 8 languages around the world.

Born and raised in Germany, Cassandra attended business school in her hometown before immigrating to America when she was only eighteen. At nineteen, she married her husband, who was active duty military at that time. Together, they traveled the country for years, before finally settling down. Now, she lives in the mountains of North Carolina with her husband of sixteen years, their three children, two dogs, and one hairless cat.
With a love for reading, that love slowly transpired into writing she put her fingers to the keyboard and started writing about the dark side of romance.

Printed in Great Britain
by Amazon